THE BLACK GUM WELL
(A Novel)

by

Carolyn Pennington

DORRANCE
PUBLISHING CO
EST. 1920
PITTSBURGH, PENNSYLVANIA 15238

Dorrance Publishing Co
585 Alpha Drive
Pittsburgh, PA 15238
Visit our website at *www.dorrancebookstore.com*

ISBN: 978-1-6461-0213-6
eISBN: 978-1-6461-0548-9

Acknowledgments

R. Wayne Pennington, J. Todd Dockery, and R. Luke Coffey

CHAPTER 1

Tine felt the baby pressing down on her back bone like an immovable black rock. The pain didn't feel like any other pain she had ever felt while she was carrying the other children. She took hold of the cow gap fence post and steadied herself as a pain shot like a streak of hot fire across her entire back. Tine let out a breath slowly and released it with the easing of the pain, lifted her apron tail and dabbed the cold beads of perspiration off her upper lip. The apron was stained in light red blotches.

Tine had worked the garden that morning and picked strawberries the best she could. The hugeness of her belly which pushed up right under her breast line forced her to squat down to pick the berries. The apron had to be awkwardly tied over her swollen belly and it rode up in front. If the baby kept on growing, her dress would be pushed up in front four inches above her knees before it was born which would be a disgrace.

Her light brown feed sack dress with little yellow flowers woven into the fabric was faded out so the flowers were barely distinguishable. She had not had time to sew anything new to wear in awhile with the garden to work in the spring. All her best dresses were much too little and wouldn't stretch across her protruding belly. Her feet wiggled around in Bentley's big brogan shoes. Tine saved her shoes and never

1

wore them out in the fields. Bentley cast his shoes off before they ever wore completely out and allowed they made good shoes for her to wear working in the garden and fields. Tine tied the shoe strings tight around the ankles and let her feet slide around inside the big shoes. At least they kept her feet off the ground, but the shoes made her even clumsier as she lumbered about trying to get the chores done.

Tine was a good looker everyone was always telling Bentley. She had never taken on weight like most women who kept on having children in their middle age. She was short but sturdy with hips just wide enough to carry babies well.

Her black Cherokee-like hair ran in her family. She grew her hair long and wadded it up in a bun on the back of her neck. Her mom had always told her that hair like hers was an extra dose of glory straight from the hand of God. The children loved it when she let her hair down at night. In fact, Susie would comb and comb her hair and say every time, "Mom, I wish I had your hair. It's the prettiest hair I've ever seen. It feels like silk!"

Tine loved the fact that she didn't have a single gray hair in her head.

Her hands were beginning to look like an old woman's hands. Hard work kept her finger nails broken and stained. Recently, Tine had noticed that the forefinger on her right hand had an arthritis knot beginning to show, and she could no longer slide her wedding ring off because the knuckle on that finger was enlarged. A woman with hands that looked as old as hers did not have any business having another baby.

Tine sat down on a fallen oak log to rest a spell. To her left, a rail fence zigzagged its way up the middle of the pasture field to the family cemetery on the top of the hill. One single oak tree left in the clearing that Bentley's dad made for the graveyard stood tall and straight like a giant finger pointing the way to heaven. On the steepest part of the hill below the flat cemetery, a grove of young popular trees grew. Their fresh lime green leaves whispered as breezes fluttered them. Tine's blue eyes with a sad like softness in them played over her surroundings. The spring sun warmed her straight and strong shoulders. Tine's arms and face were already tanned hen-egg brown from having worked outside all spring. Her skin was smooth and radiant.

Tine never wore a bonnet. Covering one's head and face while outside in the sun was something she hated, even if it were the proper thing for a woman to do.

Two tiny little yellow butterflies circled as if some invisible lasso were tied to them twirling them around in the air above a half dried up cow hoof print on the foot path. Tine sniffed the air. The early apple tree blossoms in the orchard perfumed the air ever so faintly.

The baby lurched inside her. She winced.

"What in the world is so different with this baby? You'd think that with six children already birthed this one would be a breeze," Tine muttered to herself as she picked up each five-gallon water bucket.

She continued her mid-afternoon journey along the hard ground of the rutted-out cow path around the side of the hill until the spring appeared. Christmas ferns laced each side of the ravine that hugged the spring. Moss carpeted the rocks along side the stream that let the spring wander its way to lower ground to join the small creek at the foot of the hill. A chicken hawk circled high overhead the pines seeking sight of a mid morning breakfast, a field mouse or ground squirrel, perhaps. A couple of blue jays screamed at each other in the distance.

Her head felt a bit dizzy. Tine looked again towards the house. She could only see the roof from where she stood at the entrance to the ravine. Surely the children would come looking for her if for some reason she did not make it back to the house. Her head felt a bit dizzy again.

Tine bent over and sloshed the cooling waters over her face.

Her mind flirted off in the direction of Eunice's house. Eunice, her sister-in-law, was her constant champion. They had done everything together since the time they met right after Eunice married Oscar and Bentley had married her. Tine could see as plain as day Eunice and her allowing Loy and Leonard and Sylvie and Sally, her oldest four children, splash and play in the water below the spring when they had come to the well on hot afternoons to get water before they got supper for their husbands. Eunice had lost all four of her first children during the early stages of the pregnancy. She had confided in Tine that all of a sudden the babies would just disappear with a few cramps that would come real fast like and be over. Eunice would always have to take to her bed for a week or two after the miscarriages. The family never spoke of the miscarriages except to say that Eunice had taken poorly again. Tine used to feel a tinge of guilt at how Eunice loved and played with her children for years before she had her own girls, Arleta and Arvella. Tine was the only one at Eunice's side when Arvella was born. The midwife left them after about eighteen hours of Eunice's being in labor with the ill omen that there was nothing else to do but let nature take its course. The midwife announced with conviction and authority that the baby was too big to be born to a woman with as small a frame as Eunice's.

Tine did not leave Eunice after the midwife left. She stayed by the bed and washed Eunice's face with cold rags, hour after for hour for three whole days. Eunice barely was able to ask for water now and then. Tine had held the cup of water to her lips and poured it down her throat all the time saying to Eunice in hushed tones, "You can have this one, hang on. This one is a full-term baby and I just know we can get it here. Together we can do it."

Sure enough, all of a sudden with a big lurch of pain then a release with one last hoarse scream from Eunice, that little Arvella just squirted out to the world. Tine had run like a wild turkey to Oscar and Bentley who were putting up hay in the meadow right close to the house. She went yelling every step, "The baby is here. It is here. It's a big healthy girl. Come quick!"

Tine whirled back to Eunice's bedside. She cut the cord and wrapped the baby to get her ready for Oscar to hold. She did not even bathe the baby.

Tine would never forget how Oscar cradled that little girl in his arms while he climbed right up in the bed with Eunice. He had held the baby in the crook of one arm. He had taken his free arm and crooked in behind Eunice and lifted her up to him and kissed her face all over saying, "Look Little Momma what you have done. Look Little Momma what you have done. You got us a girl. You got us a little girl baby."

Eunice was so weak, she didn't make a sound; but she gazed on Oscar's face and sent him a weak smile before he let her slide off his arm onto the bed. Eunice fell immediately to sleep as Oscar sat on the bedside and gently rocked his girl child.

Tine had walked over and lifted the baby from Oscar. She headed to the kitchen where Bentley was pouring a pitcher of cold water into a pot of hot water to cool it to a temperature right for giving the little girl her first bath. Tine had cried tears of jubilation and relief as she washed the new born before she carried her to Eunice for its first nursing.

Tine felt a tear slid down her face at the tenderness she had witnessed between Oscar and Eunice that day. She reached up with her forefinger and dabbed the tear away.

Tine broke a handful of daises and stuffed them into her apron pocket. She would get a jar of water and put them on the table when she got to the house.

On summer days when the work was all caught up, she and Eunice used to take a bucket with ham and biscuits and jelly biscuits and a dipper and make the children a picnic on the ground sometimes under a big deep shade tree close to the well. They could go get fresh water anytime they got thirsty. Tine took a big quilt to make them a pallet to play on. Eunice would weave a crown of flowers out of daises for the girls.

The girls still remembered playing with Eunice. Sally said the last time she was home that all the girls should get together and go do a dinner on the ground just like they did when she and Sylvie were little.

Tine swallowed hard. Eunice had been in the bed for about three weeks now with her baby that was due any time now. "Lord, be with her. Lord be with me, too," Tine prayed silently.

Tine thought again about that night Arleta was born.

On the way home that night, Bentley told Tine, "You are sure like a sister to Oscar and Eunice. You sure are a good woman, Tine."

Tine felt warm and good at his affirmation. She had walked on silent for fear she might burst out crying again. She needed to get to her children home from Mam's who had been keeping them while she was with Eunice.

Tine was aware that she needed to hurry back to the house. The spring never had seemed as far from the house as it did to her today as heavy with child as she was. She eased slowly down the hill towards the barn.

Bentley had carefully planned to build their house as close to the spring as he could so they would always have plenty of fresh water. His dad said in all his lifetime that the spring had always run a full steam every season even during the driest times that he could ever recall.

Tine had a habit of talking to herself when she was out working alone.

"Lord, how I miss Sally," Tine said. "I miss her so bad." The words were like a prayer. She needed Sally now.

"If this pain gets any worse, I'll have to send Bentley after her. She can help me with the other children if this baby makes me have to take to my bed. Surely, it won't come to me having to take to my bed."

She had not gone to bed but a day to have each of the other children and was right back up the next day going about and doing nearly everything she had wanted to do. Mommy and Hester, the old granny woman, had told everyone, "Tine beats anything at birthing babies." Tine was older now and this was Tine's seventh baby. Old women always were saying the older a woman is the harder the birthing is. Tine found herself about to believe them.

This baby was being so contrary. It was kicking the living daylights out of her even before it was born. She was so heavy and cumbersome that when she bent down, she could hardly move back into an upward position.

Normally, Tine was able to get all the wash done in one day; but, today it was getting late and she still needed to scrub out the sheets and hang them out before she got supper.

Tine scanned the horizon towards the corn field. She strained to listen for hoes clicking or plows making some noise or the squeaking of leather on mule harness as they pulled the plows, but she couldn't see anyone nor hear a sound of the children working the cornfield.

If they didn't get the corn all worked out before sundown when Bentley got home from his produce wagon run, he would grumble and complain until bedtime. If any one of the children said a word he did not like, he might haul off and slap the holy dickens out of any one of them.

She could hear him now. It was always the same: "Upon my honor, I cannot figure out for the life of me why you all can't turn off no more than you do when I am gone off trying to make us a few extra dollars. Looks like I may have to drop the produce run, if this is all the work that you all get done without me here a making shore it gets done fast and right."

His body would be tense when he talked; his arms would be at his sides with stiffness in his elbows. The space between his eyes would be wrinkled tight. The dark of his eyes would be focused out in space like he was looking at something only he could see. He never did look directly at one of them while he was ranting and raving.

Tine never answered his complaints nor did the children. They all would stay quiet until he defeated himself. He would get stuck and go over the same old thing, word for word. Both she and the children knew that there was no way that Bentley would give up his produce wagon route. He made more money than anyone else in their valley.

Bentley never told Tine or the children how much money he made. He always just said, "I'm saving the money for hard times." Tine thought she knew though where he had buried the money in glass jars down by the cane mill.

About every Saturday, when the weather was warm, she would see him go down that way with a gallon molasses jar and shovel, stay awhile and then come back. He would put the shovel back in the barn and come on to the house about the edge of dark and never say a word.

"I know I can find and dig up a thing as big as a molassy jar," she would say to herself when she pondered such things.

Another sharp pain struck her right across her back straight over her hips. She set the buckets down so she could rest. She straightened up and rubbed the small of her back. The pain went away.

"I swear, I don't know whether I can get these buckets back to the house and finish washing the sheets or not," she explained again.

This baby was riding on her tail bone like an iron wedge. She hoped it had not dropped, though the thought made her worry. It was not due for at least three weeks to a month.

"I am as clumsy and awkward as one of them old cows about ready to calf," she half laughed, hoping to fling the worry from her mind. Anyways the Bible says that God has given man power over all that he had made on earth. I can't help but wonder how come God did not give women much power, especially over how many children would come."

"I'm almost forty two years old. Some women have them to forty five or even fifty, which is too old if you ask me to have a baby to raise."

Fear flowed in her chest as her mind tried to sort out her predicament.

Tine muttered, "I am so tired of having children, but the Lord promised not to put anything on me that I can't bear. Surely this will be the last one."

With both buckets evenly balanced, Tine plodded slowly down the path back closer to the house. She placed her feet carefully as she started down the slope to the branch where the water had nearly dried up.

Puddles of cow pie and green slimy algae lay in silent pools of hardened mud-rimmed puddles. Tad poles were darting around in a few of the puddles that were not too stagnated to support their lives.

8

As she inched down slope she wondered if Eunice had been feeling like her baby was as close to being born as this one did. Their babies were supposed to come at about the same time, the best they could tell. It was getting awful close to the full of the moon. Everybody knew more babies were born on the full of the moon than at any other time. Tine wished she felt like going out to Eunice's house to sit with her awhile.

Tine felt dizzy. Silver spots like little balls of light danced in front of her eyes. She stopped and set the buckets down on a level spot and tried to focus her eyes. She reached to get the bucket handles. Her own hot water streamed down both her legs. Tine looked again toward the field, but there was not a sound or a sight. She started to hasten her steps. If she made it to the house, the children would find her when they got home. She felt her knees buckle.

She rolled like a sack of potatoes towards the branch and landed in the largest pool of branch water. Her water, streaked with blood, oozed into the murky water of the half dried up stream. Tad poles scurried in fright straight up her legs and hid in the folds of her bloomers.

CHAPTER 2

Tine woke up. She could not remember where she had been or what she had been doing. She had had a big long dream about her and Bentley's gets married. She had not thought of her wedding day in years with all the work and babies. Tine's head cleared a bit. She felt tugs on both her breasts.

"How come I have babies at my breasts?" She fumbled out the words in confused tones as she glanced down at two nursing babies. One infant was a big robust baby boy on her right breast. On her left breast was a tiny fragile blue looking little baby girl. The big baby was nursing hard and fast, and the little one lipped her nipple in a weak and labored manner was just barely able to squeeze a bit of a little milk.

Tine's vision was blurry. She shook her head to focus her eyes. There, she could see now. She saw the early morning soft pink light filter through the east window to her bed room. She knew she was at home.

She recalled trying to get from the spring to the house because she knew the baby had decided to come. She remembered falling at that milk gap branch. She wrinkled her brow in a frown trying to recall what had happened to her after she had fallen.

From the dingy far corner of the bedroom, a voice startled her.

"Tine, you are okay and your baby is okay? You were out through the whole birthing. Bentley and the children thought shore to God that you were going to die and leave them. Your labor was three days before you got him here. He is a big boy, nearly eleven pounds. You both are a doing fine. We all knew you'd come back sooner or later. You are a strong woman, Tine. You will get your strength back. Just lay real quiet and let the rest of us take good care of you and the babies. The little one is mine."

Tine recognized the smooth soothing voice of her husband's brother, Oscar.

She remembered Eunice. Fear entered her mind.

She swallowed hard, then, blurted out, "Where is Eunice? This little girl is her baby, ain't it?"

Tine began to choke up.

Oscar did not answer her question, but went on, "Tine, you scared us all to death; even that granny-woman told Bentley that if you ever had another baby you might not make it through."

He paused, swallowed hard, and then spoke in an even kind but flat tone, "Tine, we buried Eunice yesterday. I had to bring my little baby to you to nurse so she would not die, too. Bentley, thank God, got her to nurse you even with you out."

Oscar caught a deep breath and continued, "Bentley is gone on the produce run. He has been by your bed ever minute since your baby boy was born until today. He asked me to sit with you while he went to work. The people that buy off the wagon wouldn't understand if he did not come on after not being there for them to buy over a week now. They depend on him for eggs and chickens for sure."

The children are all gone to school. I had to stay here with you and the babies. Dr. Jed was here yesterday and he said you would pull out of it."

Oscar ceased talking and did not move; he just stared blankly and wide eyed into space.

Tine just lay and sobbed as she looked down at the babies.

Oscar slid out of his chair in the corner and came to her bedside. He lifted his miniature baby up from Tine's side and wrapped her up in the blanket. He walked around and around holding her to his chest for a good while; then, he eased the girl baby down on her stomach in the cradle. He went to Tine's other side and repeated the procedure for her boy baby and placed him in the crib beside Tine's bed.

"There, there, you little Johnny boy," Oscar comforted the baby.

"Ahh," Tine muttered, in a half asleep weak voice, "I did not have a name picked out for him and Bentley didn't either. I'll just tell Bentley that his name is John Oscar, and we will call him Johnny. Bentley will like that name. He will like it that I have named him after you."

Oscar moved into the living room by the fireplace and sat in the rocking chair.

Oscar laid his head back on the back of the chair and drifted off to sleep. The two babies slept, too.

Oscar had been up for the most of the last five days. Nature demanded that he sleep. His body and his soul were raw. His wife was dead. His little girls had no mother. His baby was barely breathing.

CHAPTER 3

Callie breathed her last breath at 2:10 pm. Tine was holding her. When Tine realized that the baby was dead, she gently laid her into her crib and pulled the sheet up over her miniature chalk-like doll face.

Oscar stood beside Tine and watched her place the dead child down. They did not speak. In slow motion towards the kitchen as if driven by instinct, they went.

No tears flowed from either of them.

Oscar bent over and picked up a log from the stove wood box in and stirred up the fire with the end of it before he dropped it into the fire. Tine lifted the lid off the reservoir of warm water and filled a pan large enough to bathe the deceased child. She vacated the room and went into the other part of the house in search of sheets and towels to use to lay out the child.

Oscar did not bend up completely after he had dropped the piece of wood and let the lid back down on the stove over the fire. He kept his eyes upon his feet as he inched over to the table. He placed his hands on the table and let himself down into a chair. He sat with his gaze upon the floor. His shoulders slumped and his hands limp in his lap.

Tine returned with a white sheet and two towels folded and hanging over her left arm. She carried a white crocheted dress and cap for

Callie to wear as her burial gown clutched in her right hand. She put the dress and cap in a chair beside the table. She bit her trembling lower lip as she spread the sheet on the small kitchen table. She folded the sheet into a small rectangle before laying it down on the table as a pad for the dead child. She moved to the stove and trilled her fingers in the pan of warm water resting on the stove.

She did not look at Oscar as she almost whispered, "The water is ready," while she was bending over the table smoothing the wrinkles out of the sheet as if she were making a bed.

"I will go get her," she said.

Oscar choked out, "I don't think I can touch her yet to save my life. I don't think that I can stand it. Give me another minute or two."

Tine went into the side room, stood for a moment looking down at the sheet-covered crib. She took a deep sharp breath and scooped the still warm baby into her arms. Her hands trembled as the baby's head rolled around on her arm. Tine took her free hand and held its little head secure so that her head would not bob around as she walked carrying the baby to rest again on the center of the kitchen table. The baby's finger nails were blue, and a blue ring encircled its mouth.

Tine placed the baby on the center of the kitchen table gently, ever so gently. She positioned the baby's head on the table until it lay stationary.

Oscar gazed at Tine intently with a sad, grateful fondness in his eyes.

Tine took the cloth and wet it in the warm water. She began to wash the baby's body in little brush-like strokes much like that of a momma cat's when licking her kitten.

"I will dress her for the burial," Tine informed Oscar in a level tone.

Tine had an urge to scream out in pain; but, instead, she just went right on staying calm and quiet for Oscar's sake. She knew that he was hurting worse than he showing. Her own guts wrenched so hard with grief that she looked down to see if her belly were shaking through her apron. She would go cry it out in the barn loft or somewhere all alone after the funeral was over and the baby buried.

After Tine finished the washing ritual, ever so carefully, she dried the baby's still and cold fragile body. She dressed the pale bluish baby in the little white dress. She slipped the little crocheted cap with the embroidered pink flowers on Callie; then, she tied the ribbon in a bow under her little chin.

Tine started to place Callie back on the center of the table. Oscar pointed the fingers of his right hand into the air in a gesture to stop her. He held out both his arms as a signal that he wanted to hold his deceased child.

Oscar lifted the limp little body and laid her up on his shoulder. He took his right hand and braced the back of her head and neck as he would have a live child. Oscar eased down to sit into the four-legged bark-bottomed chair. He began to rock back and forth in the four post chair that clicked out a heavy pounding of a rhythm back and forth from the two front legs unto the back two legs. The clicking of the chair legs beat out in the silence a staid eerie rhythmic rocking pattern. After the second or third rock, Oscar began to moan out unintelligible groans of grief in unison with the beats of the chair legs on the floor.

He cradled the child on his chest as he rocked her, "I don't know how I can stand this without Eunice."

CHAPTER 4

Honey bees were working the short clover in the newly mown graveyard grasses.

"Suffer little children to come unto me…"Preacher Johnson was drumming out in a monotone voice. "Dust to dust," the preacher was saying just like he did at every graveside.

The inside of Tine's head screamed, "I couldn't save her."

Oscar whispered into Bentley's ear. He picked up each of his little girls' hands. He led them to the side of the casket. He lifted them, one on each arm, and allowed them a view of their little sister in her casket. Each child gazed ever so slightly upon the corpse then turned and hid their faces on their father's shoulders.

Tine felt spasms undulating in her stomach as she gazed upon the tiny bit of a child, Callie. The colors of the trip-around-the-world quilt of Callie's funeral shroud were blurry streaks of color through her teary eyes. She and Eunice had decided to make identical quilts for their new babies and had put yellows, blues, greens and other colors so the quilts would be good for a boy or a girl either one.

Tine felt a tinge of guilt that she had her boy and he was alive and wrapped in his quilt.

Her mouth quivered.

Tine let her breath out in a lurch as she slipped her arm ever so lightly around Oscar's back. His face was buried into his handkerchief. His entire body was shaking in uncontrollable sobs. The girls were hanging onto his pant's legs, one on each side with fear clouding their eyes.

Bentley let his hand go from Oscar's elbow and laid his arm around the shoulders of his brother to steady him as Oscar wobbled on his knees. After a minute or two, Oscar drew himself up somewhat straighter. Bentley abruptly left Oscar to stand alone. He crossed the graveyard and headed in the direction where the waiting mules were tired up to a sprawling oak tree.

One of the women from the church broke out in a clear sweet voice into a clear melody, "I will meet you in the morning by the bright river side…" Her music drifted across the hilltops and seemed to hang over the valley in hopeful echoes before it ceased. At the end of the song, Oscar turned to Tine and spoke.

"Let's go. Bentley has brought the wagon up to the gate. I just need to take my girls and go to my house where we can cry. Will you come to the house with us for a little while? You and Bentley? I don't think I can stand to have another soul about me but you and him and my girls."

Tine could feel the streams of milk oozing out her nipples from her full breasts.

Tine answered, "I need to stop by the house to feed Johnny. Then, I can come on out and get the girls all settled in and feed them their supper before I have to get back to the house to Susie and Johnny. Bentley can stay as long as you want. Susie can do all the chores without him."

Tine took hold of little Arleta's hand and Oscar's eyes pierced into hers as if he could not turn away from her. Oscar took Arleta's hand and Arvella's hand, one on each side of him. The little girls' faces were perplexed. Oscar, his girls, and Tine crossed the grass to the gate where Bentley awaited them. Bentley climbed down off the wagon and lifted the girls over the side boards. He placed them on a quilt. He took another quilt and wrapped it around them to keep the wind off their backs.

Nobody spoke a word.

Bentley took Tine's elbow and hoisted her unto the wagon seat beside him. Tine reached out her white gloved hand to Oscar and pulled him unto the wagon seat beside her. Oscar smiled a weak sad smile.

Bentley clucked to the mules and slapped the reigns. The wagon wheels rolled and squeaked as if they, too, were wounded by Callie's death. Tine kept her right hand on Oscar's arm and her left one on Bentley's right on the forearm that shifted gently to instruct the mules as needed.

Oscar and Bentley stared straight ahead. Tine looked down from Oscar's face that was one single grimace of grief. Bentley's mouth quivered.

Chapter 5

The girl baby, Callie, had been in her grave for almost a month. Tine chocked back a tear as she looked up the hill toward the family cemetery. Oscar and Bentley's dad started the family burial plot when his first child died at four years old with the fever. It wasn't too long after that that Elmer, his son, had died at just twenty eight years old. Elmer died before she and Bentley married. There were four graves upon the hill now that Eunice and the baby in freshly covered graves were alongside them.

Tine still felt Callie in bed when she woke up in the middle of the night to feed Johnny. When she was nursing Oscar's baby for him it was like having twins. One of the babies wanted its milk almost all the time. Tine had put them both in the bed with her, one on one side and one on the other. She did not have enough strength after all her loss of blood during the long labor to get up and down and nurse the babies. She needed rest more than anything. Tine frowned. Try as she might, she still could not remember anything about having birthed Johnny.

She missed Eunice. She wondered how in the world she could get all the beans canned without her. She could not bear the thought of ever quilting a quilt again since Eunice would not be there to help her sew away the long winter days.

Tine was numb and lonely. The image of Callie's little lips and tiny little fingers and toes that had stayed bluish looking the whole time that she was nursing her seemed stuck in Tine's mind.

Tine frowned in a grimace of headache pain. Her eyes got blurry now when the pain was the worst. Her head hurt all day sometimes. The strong sun rays penetrating right through her bonnet seemed to make her head hurt worse. Today the pain was a dull throb instead of the sharp pains she usually had.

Balls of steel colored light flashed in her eyes for seconds off and on. She couldn't find a pattern to the pain and lights flashing in her eyes like stars blinking. The balls of light just appeared and disappeared without warning.

Tine thought to herself, "I wonder what this headache and blurry eye stuff I keep having is all about. Maybe it is from me having had a hard time with Johnny's being born and losing Eunice. Maybe I am a feeling bad because I can't cry over Eunice's and Callie's death to save me."

Today was the first time she had been back to the spring from that day she fell and went into labor with Johnny. The rest of the family was off in the fields working. Bentley was on his produce run. Susie was out at Mam's which was just down the dirt road a piece around the curve of the hill. She could see Mam's back yard. No was out there helping Mam. Mam wasn't able to bend over and pick beans anymore, so Tine had sent Susie to help her work even though it was hard to spare her.

Tine had left Johnny asleep in his bed. She had her strength up enough to go get a bucket of water from the spring and get back to the house with it before the baby woke up. If Johnny did wake up before she got back with the water, it wouldn't hurt him to cry a little until she got back to the house.

As she sat on the bucket, her eyes cleared. She looked down the valley over the garden toward Oscar's house. No one was stirring there. Mam and Susie must be in the house canning the beans.

Tine pondered over her daughters while she rested. She was proud of her Susie, who at thirteen, could already keep a house and a garden and take care of a family. She would make a good wife and mother. Sally was a good wife but there were no signs of a baby with her yet. Some women took a lot longer to get in the family way than others.

"Lord, I hope my days of having babies are over especially if I get in such bad shape that I nearly die and can't remember having this child for the life of me," she breathed to herself, almost shocked at her thoughts.

She took a deep breath and stood up, steadied herself with one hand on the locust fence post, picked up a ripe apple and bit into its soft mellowness. The apples had begun to let go and fall off which meant she and Susie would have to start gathering them every day to work them up into jelly and can and dry them. She picked up her empty bucket and started on up the sloped cow path to the spring.

In the ravine where the spring was centered, mushrooms and lacy moss hung along the edges of the bank. Shadow-loving wild flowers would swing and flaunt their blossoms upside down from the heavy black moist earth along the sides of the back above the black gum drum when the eternal spout of water spewed out. The black gum tree spring was such a stout stream that besides never going dry, it never ever froze completely over even on the coldest winter day. The place stood in silence except for the tingling splashes of invitation from the eternal spring to come and sit and drink.

A pair of cardinals hung onto a hemlock branch as she slipped off the path into the hollow towards the spring. One day in the chicken lot she had noticed a male cardinal in the spring while nesting taking a little piece of corn and turning his head sideways and slipping that grain of corn right into his female partner's mouth. It was something real special to see a male cardinal expressing his love for his little mate living life the way it ought to be lived.

Bubbles of perspiration had popped out on her forehead. Tine lifted her dress tail and wiped the sweat off her face. The humidity hung heavy like an invisible soggy blanket in the darkness of the little ravine that encased the spring. Gnats and an occasional mosquito darted at her hot face. She pulled off her bonnet and slapped them away.

She knelt down on her knees in front of the overflowing streams of water that was bouncing off the edges of the black gum tree and streaming down the sides. She cupped her hands and sloshed big handfuls of water over her face. She untied her apron and dried off her face and hung the apron and bonnet on a low pine branch to dry.

She sat down in the pine needles. Tine did not have to hurry; Johnny would sleep an hour or two at a time now. She lifted her skirt up above her knees to let the cool air surround her naked legs. The dank earth felt cool to her bare legs on the hot day. Tine lay back and looked up at the pristine clear sky with light white clouds that danced across the sky. The bits of sunlight that filtered down through the overlapping pine branch needles made light patterns on the ground like a crazy quilt's patterns. Chickadees pecked on the pine cones and flitted from one cone to another one gathering bites of the cones for themselves as they shifted from pine cone to pine cone. Tine delighted in watching them go about their day's work in such a delicate and sweet unhurried way.

Tine thought she heard something move on the hill through the thick woods behind her. She sat up straight and started to get up. All of a sudden behind her, she heard footsteps coming around the side of the hill on the path towards the spring. Oscar's voice appeared just as he did. Tine yanked her dress tail back down over her knees.

"Why Tine what are you doing out here in the middle of this hot day by yourself? Don't get up from resting. Are you sure you ought to be out here this soon with you being down as long as you had to be with them babies pulling on you like they done?" He offered the questions falling one after another as he plodded up the hill side path towards her.

Tine caught her breath. She had not seen him since the baby's funeral.

26

Tine's throat got tight when she remembered how she had moved slowly across the kitchen floor and had put her hands on Oscar's shoulders when he was rocking his little dead Callie in his arms. She had rubbed and rubbed his shoulders and the back of his neck while he bent over the child cuddling her against his chest.

Oscar had risen from the chair and had moved as if in a stupor and followed her. In the side bedroom, Tine had placed the deceased baby back into the cradle. She then pulled the quilt up over her face as if to hide the reality of her death from them.

When she had turned to go back to the kitchen, Oscar had reached out and then had pulled her toward him. She had leaned into his chest; they both had begun to shake with conjoined grief that had came in surges in their bodies. Callie had felt to Tine just like she had been her baby, too, after she had nursed her.

"Are you all out of water?" Tine asked Oscar as he plopped down beside her and set his two large wooden buckets down.

"No, but the well is running low at my house because Mam used so much water out her well for her and Susie to do the canning. When I went to get water from her well, she sent me around the hill to your and Bentley's spring. Mam was afraid they might draw the well plum dry if they did not slow down and give it time to fill up again."

"It never entered my head that you would be here getting water," Oscar stated in an even tone. He filled his buckets by letting them set on the rock below the streams of water and fill themselves.

He did not speak as the buckets filled themselves and neither did Tine. After Oscar set the filled and running over buckets aside, he moved back over to Tine and sat down beside her again. They sat side by side for a few silent moments.

Tine yearned to touch him. Oscar's eyes were tired looking. His shoulders were slightly stooped. He sat with his hands on his knees. His shirt was rolled up to his elbows and his bibbed overalls held a can of Prince Albert smoking tobacco that protruded out of the unzipped little holding pocket on the bib. He did not take out the tobacco and white tissue papers and roll a cigarette to smoke. He stared up the hill at the little cemetery.

Oscar broke the silence. "I done a big wash this morning and hung it out," Oscar chuckled and said, "I just can't seem to do this house stuff very good. I'm as clumsy as a cow in a rail pile especially when I try to cook and do kitchen work. It takes me nearly twice as long to wash and hang the clothes as it used to Eunice. I have found out that I ain't much at woman's work. Every man ought to have to take care of two little girls and keep house for just one week; they would learn that woman's work ain't easy. He might decide he has the easiest job in the world."

Tine laughed deep in her throat. It tickled her to death to hear a man say such a thing.

Oscar reached over and took a hold of her hand with real gentle like movement. He spoke gently in an almost whispered voice, "I have missed coming out and setting with you since the baby died. I appreciate you, Tine."

Tine trembled at the softness in his voice.

She did not withdraw her hand.

"Well, I needed you to help me, too, Oscar. I did not have a soul to talk to and I miss Sally something awful since she married off. The other children are always out and gone to fields. The boys go off to court or hunt or something as soon as supper's over. I miss Mom and Carlista, too, since I married Bentley and moved off over her on the branch. Bentley is gone from before daylight until after dark. He drops dead into sleep as soon as he eats his supper and goes to bed."

Oscar lifted her hand to his lips and barely caressed her fingers with a light kiss on the top.

Tine did not pull away.

"Tine, I don't think I could have walked to the funeral of my baby girl without you standing on one side of me and Bentley on the other.

It was you that I got my strength from. Bentley was not much help he was so tore up that he almost lost you the way I did Eunice. He told me out at the house on the front porch other night that he didn't think he could have stood it had he a lost you or little Johnny either one, much less both. He told me that he was so hurt for me that he couldn't cry a tear his heart was busting so much. He said he vowed to God over in the crib on his knees in the shelled corn that he would not ever put you in a position to take a chance on you having to birth another baby. He is afraid that he might lose you."

Tine replied, "Well, he has not said one word to me about anything except that he'll try to be back home before dark ever night and will be if there is no unexpected trouble on his produce run. He sure stays off to hisself; he is always at the barn or out somewhere."

Oscar still was a hold of her hand.

He stood up and pulled Tine up beside him.

When Tine was on her feet, he pulled her toward him; she eased her head into his chest. Tine let her arms slide around him while he encircled her with his long gangly arms. He took one hand and tasseled the hair on the back of her head.

Tine kept her head lying against his chest. She could hear his heart racing underneath the bib of his overalls. She felt her own heart racing. They stood embraced for several minutes; then, Oscar squeezed her so tightly and kissed the top of her head as he released her. Tine knew his hardness against her belly. She knew he was so hungry for a woman. Tine knew she was going to try to be at the spring every day after the mid-day meal's dishes were washed up.

"Tine, it gives me a pleasure to have your company a few minutes out here in the cool and the quiet. It helps me to get out by myself a few minutes more and walk in the woods." Oscar gazed softy into Tine's eyes as he spoke.

Abruptly he turned from her and picked up his water buckets. He started back down the path to his mother's house.

Tine picked up her buckets and each one of them started back carrying their heavy loads.

They did not look back.

Black-eyed Susans and golden rod graced the sides of the cow path. Tine eased along the hilly path under the spreading oaks, maples, and poplars that made a dark shade to travel beneath and keep her cool on her trek back home.

She stumped her toe and water sloshed over the edges of her bucket. She slowed to a more deliberate placing of her feet. She sure did not want to spill her water and have to go back for more in this blazing sun. She hoped Johnny was still asleep. Tine felt a tinge of guilt in her joy at a meeting up with Oscar. She had all but forgotten about the baby.

Tine had not thought about her being Bentley's wife and Oscar's being Bentley's brother or nothing like that while Oscar was holding her. It seemed to be just natural to be with Oscar like he was her best friend even if he were a man.

CHAPTER 6

It was early August. The crops were laid by. Susie was busy sewing up new dresses and aprons and bonnets out of dairy feed sacks. A girl had to have clothes ready for being a wife who could stay prettied up even when she was at home working.

Johnny could eat a little soft table food now and did not have to be nursed very often. Actually, he got by with just a morning feeding and an evening feeding before Tine put him down for the night. Oscar's girls went to their grandma's house every afternoon and helped get supper for their grandpa and Oscar.

Oscar needed water almost everyday in the dry hot weather and so did Tine.

Today, Oscar and Tine were at the spring and in no hurry to leave. The spring holler was cool. A mist sometimes rose from the splashes of overflowing water. Oscar and Tine sat next to each other on a big rock beside the stream below the well drum.

Tine had pulled her shoes off and was dancing her toes in the cool stream. Oscar pulled his shirt off and laid it on the rock for them to sit on. His back was golden brown from plowing in the fields all summer without a shirt. Tine rubbed his tanned shoulder and back with her right hand.

"Oscar, tell me about your brother who died. Bentley never has said much about him even though he had not been dead too awful long before we started courtin'. All he ever said was that Elmer was a puny child and he was a right puny man and stayed right sickly until that double pneumonia got him that winter right after Christmas."

Oscar leaned back on one elbow and took his homemade sassafras tooth pick out of his mouth. "I don't remember him much when I was a child. He was always playing with animals, but he did not like a horse or a mule. He grew tame rabbits of every kind. He kept a litter of kittens around and pups, too. He never did learn to ride horses like the rest of us boys. He would not plow no matter what Pap said or did. Mam used to get mad enough at him to kill him."

Oscar chuckled at the memory.

"He would slip kittens in upstairs and sleep with them. Mam would catch Elmer out gone; she'd fill up a coffee sack with kittens and take them a way down the creek to a big water hole. Then would add a big rock in the sack and sink them kittens away. It never did no good. The first thing you know, Elmer would bring in a big old momma cat and kittens from somewhere else."

Oscar chuckled again remembering his Mom's furor at those kittens.

He continued, "Elmer had lambs and whatever else he could raise. He had him a pet raccoon and a pet possum, too. I believe it was rabbits he liked the best. Mam did allow him to have one big old white house rabbit in his room. Elmer called him 'Snowball.'"

Tine asked, "Did he have a girlfriend anytime?"

Oscar replied, "He never did have a woman of any kind in all his twenty nine years, but he was real good friends with Freddie Hammonds and his mommy. He never did go off the place except to walk that five miles or so to their house."

The sinking sun warned Oscar and Tine to end their time together and head back to their houses before time to get supper.

Oscar and Tine met often all summer on easy afternoons. Kisses turned to fondling and fondling turned to love making. They buried themselves in each other upon the mossy bed below the spring. Often they turned and splashed themselves off in the cooling waters before they set out back to their homes and children.

When summer passed and eased into fall, on warm afternoons Oscar and Tine would simply lay holding each other on the rock, kissing and lingering in the afternoon sun allowing the sweetness of the sun and of each other to pass into their very souls.

Late fall came and their trips to the spring were less frequent.

CHAPTER 7

Oscar brought his girls to Tine and Bentley's house for Halloween. Oscar had let them cut holes in old sheets for eyes and drape the sheets over them like ghosts. Tine was so pleased that Oscar let the girls have fun. That little Arvella had been working like a grown woman ever since she was knee high to a duck.

Both the girls giggled as they came through the front door and said in unison "Wooooooh——we twin ghosts!" They repeated the line two or three times.

Then Arleta, piped, "'Trick or Treat,' and we want some of your sweet bread cookies, Tine."

Tine put some extra on a plate for them. When she came back into the living room, the girls had taken off their ghost sheets, and were taking time about with the same question.

"Did you know us? Did you know us? Daddy helped us make us something to dress up in and the ghosts were the easiest things to do."

Susie said, "You let your shoes show right out from under the sheets; so, I thought I recognized your shoes, both of you, but I wasn't positive."

Bentley humored them good by saying, "Well, I swear to my name you half scared me to death! I started to run right out that back door without a coat or anything and its cold out tonight. I thought shore something had come after me twice when I saw two ghosts just alike."

Arleta questioned him, "Didn't you see Daddy out there under them maple trees a waiting for you all to open the door after we knocked?"

Bentley replied, "Why no, you scared me so bad, I was so certain you were real ghosts, I never even thought of looking for anybody else. Jip never barked a bark either and he is a good watch dog. Shoot, a dog can't see a ghost was the reason I figured you was for real since he didn't even let out a low growl on the front porch where he always lays right there in front of the door."

But Oscar's youngest little girl answered, "Uncle Bentley, Jip smelled us is why he didn't bark or growl. He just stood there wagging his tail off and tried to lick my face, but he couldn't with me having my ghost outfit hiding my face."

Tine's eyes roamed the room and rested on Oscar. He was laughing with Bentley and the girls and Susie. It did Tine good to see him smile. He always smiled at her when she met him in the woods beside the spring when they lay down and talked and rubbed all over each other. He would start by letting her long black locks of hair down.

Bentley never did that.

She let her own hair down before she climbed in bed every night. Bentley would not have noticed if she slept with her hair all wigged up. Tine felt the burn inside herself to have Oscar a hold of her. He would kiss the back of her neck, almost like a butterfly flitting along. He would move to her jaw line and dot the entire jaw line with soft like brushes of kisses until he found her lips.

Tine wondered why Bentley is all the years they had been married and all the times he had made love to her that he just had given her a hard smack on the lips. It always felt like Oscar listened to what her body needed. Bentley did not seem to even be aware that she was down there under him. After it was over, Oscar, would just lie there all still in the pine needles. He would take a pine needle and tickle her face and the back of her neck. That sweetness made her feel warm and loved. He didn't say much, but he would hold her and rub his hands up and down her back.

Bentley looked up at Tine and jerked her out of her thoughts by saying, "Why not bring them girls a big glass a sweet milk to go with their sweet stuff? Make a pot of coffee for me and Oscar. No need to be in a hurry now that crops are laid by set us up awhile. Or better yet, Oscar, just stay the night with us. The girls can sleep with Susie. That side room has a good half bed in there. Since the boys are all gone from home, nobody ever sleeps in there. You could rest real good in there all by yourself. You ain't took a night with us since you and Eunice first got married."

Tine glanced at Oscar. It wouldn't bother her a bit for the little girls to stay, but she didn't believe she could stand to have Oscar asleep in the house.

Oscar answered Bentley, but stole a glance at Tine as if he had read her mind; he said, "I will take a cup of coffee while the children eat their sweets and drank their milk and play with Susie a bit, but we will have to get back. I don't want the fire to go out. I need to be out there early in the morning to check on them two brindle cows. Both of them are past due calving. I need to keep a close eye on them. That little one had trouble with her last calf. I can't afford to lose her or her calf. In fact, I will need to check my heifers again before I go to bed."

Tine shot him a weak smile and dismissed herself. I will get your coffee on. I have things to take care of in the kitchen. I'll bring you all out some coffee soon as it's done."

"Lay us some of that good molassy bread on a plate, too, Tine. Oscar needs something sweet to eat every once in a while since he don't have a woman to take care of him since Eunice died."

When Tine reappeared in the living room with the hot coffee and a plate of her molassy bread, Bentley informed her, "Me and Oscar was just talking and said we like to play a prank someway on the neighbors.

Oscar had the girls stop and show off their ghosts to all the family and neighbors before they got to our house which Oscar had planned to be their last stop at plum dark.

Go in there and get Susie to dress up like a boy. Oscar, you are tall and thin, so, let's have Tine get out some old clothes of hers. We can stuff you some titties. You can wear women's rubber boots without your shoes over your feet. Get him a couple pairs of cotton stockings and some garters to hold them up with so he will look just like a big tall woman and still keep his feet warm. See if you can find a bonnet that nobody will recognize; tie it real tight under his chin. Pull that bonnet brim way down low over your eyes, Oscar, so as they can't see you. You are real clean-shaved and that will help us to pass you off as a woman, too."

Oscar threw back his head and just roared with laughs. "They will never figure us out with you so short a man and me so tall a woman and with Susie's being a boy instead of a girl. I like this. I really like this. We have time to go several houses. We won't go in so they can't get a real good look at us. Come on let's practice. Bentley you talk way down low in your throat in a bass voice. I will talk real high and fine and shrill like some nervous woman. Susie, you just allow me and your 'new' daddy to do all the talking. If any of them get to quizzing you too much, I'll just say, 'Leave our child alone.' He can't hear no good and can't talk but very little. His mommy and his daddy are the only ones who can understand what he does try to say. Now, Bentley, you stick to the same story. Let's don't botch it up no way. They'll try to figure us out forever. Let's no a one of us breathe a word of this prank to a soul. We'll tell the girls to keep it under their hats, too, or they'll get in trouble. They better not breathe this prank to a soul, not even to Grandma and Grandpa."

Bentley got up and said, "I am going out to the smoke house to see what old coat and hat and boots I can find. I will turn that old ragged overcoat wrong side out not a one will recognize it."

38

Susie jumped up and down with glee. She was excited to be a boy all dressed up in her older brother's old clothes and go with her daddy and Uncle Oscar. The men didn't take girls out with them very often. She didn't even care to go away and leave and let Oscar's girls watch after Johnny and play with him.

Tine returned from the side room and looked at Oscar. He grabbed a hug from Tine while Bentley was gone to the smoke house and the children were playing down in the lower room. Tine blushed and pushed him away. She giggled like a young girl and announced, "Here are the woman's clothes. Go in the side room and put this skirt and stockings on, then come back. I will help you with your bonnet. I found this old cloak. We can turn it inside out, too. Here's a pair of old gloves that you can use to cover up your hairy fingers. Just wear your shirt. The cloak will hide it."

On his way out of the room with cotton stockings hung over one arm and a pair of garters in his hand and a long skirt slung over one arm, Oscar brushed the top of Tine's head with a kiss. She caught her breath. She rushed away from him into the living room.

Tine sat down in a chair and waited for the men and Susie to come in all dressed up and ready to go out as pranksters on Halloween.

When Bentley and Oscar came in the living room, Oscar was hanging on to Bentley's arm, standing a full foot taller than Bentley. Oscar had gone ahead and tied the bonnet and put on her woman's rubber boots. He just had socks on in the boots because his feet were so much bigger than Tine's; his shoes would not fit in the boots at all. There wasn't a way in the world anybody could have told that they were Oscar and Bentley. Tine couldn't believe her eyes at how like a husband and wife they looked. The girls and little Johnny came in clapping their hands at what a good looking boy Susie has turned out to be.

Susie had already begun playing deaf and dumb and never opened her mouth not even to laugh when Bentley said, "Now, Woman and Boy of mine, we'd better get on down the road. It won't do for us to be out late."

Oscar and Susie and Bentley went out of the house just laughing and laughing at their prank they were going to pull on all the folks they could in the neighborhood.

The little fake Halloween family returned about three hours later laughing still. "Not a soul recognized us," they reported almost in one voice.

After they got their costumes off, Oscar left carrying the girls, one on each arm. Bentley said to Oscar, "Keep your ears open and I will too, and we will find out what they all will be saying about that big tall skinny woman, that little short man, and their little deaf mute child that went around knocking on doors on Halloween. Let's go right along with them and say they come to our houses, too, and we could not figure out who in this world they were."

"Now, we all had us a good time tonight, didn't we?" Bentley added in an echo of an afterthought.

Tine answered quietly, "Yeah, we did. Every last one of us did."

Chapter 8

On a bright warm day in early November, Tine lingered at the black gum well for a while. She lay back on the rock, and allowed the sun to tease her by warming her enough that she pulled off her sweater.

Oscar appeared in no time at all. He leveled himself down beside her. He gently reached up his hand and pulled a loose stand of Tine's hair back behind her ear. He kissed the top of her ear with the delicacy of a butterfly sucking a tad of nectar off a bright orange summer butterfly weed.

Tine said to Oscar, "I keep wondering about Elmer and Freddie. Tell me more about them. It's about the time of year Elmer died. Bentley was talking a little bit about the time he died just the other day."

"That Freddie was left on the door step over at Mt. Freedom Church the day of the Christmas play. Old Preacher Johnson went early to build a fire in the stove. He found the basket with a boy baby on the step all wrapped up in blankets. The baby was no more than a day or two old they said. Well, the preacher took him into the back of the church and did not tell anyone about finding him until the end of the Christmas play. Then, he brought the basket out and held it up right and showed the whole crowd the baby boy right before the dismissing prayer. The whole crowd could not believe their eyes. They said that the preacher told the congregation that the Lord had give them this boy baby child. He asked if anybody knew a thing about the baby or why he was left there."

Oscar stopped talking and stared out into the woods before he resumed his story.

"There was a note in this baby boy's basket that said, 'Take him. I don't want him.' That is what Mam told me once. I was just a little bit of a boy, but, I remember it just like it was yesterday. There ain't never been anything like that around here before or since. To this day, not a soul knows a thing about where who left him. The preacher was dumbfounded is what Mam said. He just stood there and prayed awhile and finally said, 'Will any of you be willing to take this baby until we can find out more about this or figure out who left him?' That is what the word around here has always been," Oscar finished the narrative.

After a few minutes he began again, "It seems like whoever left him had to be someone who figgered they'd find him afore nightfall. Almost all his crazy drawings had a rabbit of some kind in them. Most folks think Freddie was not all right, but they don't ever say that."

Tine in a surprised tone stated, "Bentley never told me a bit of this."

At that Oscar grew silent. A rabbit rounded the bend of the path on the way to get her a drink. She stopped and stared at Tine and Oscar all stretched out on that rock. In a flash it darted right back into the woods like a fox evading a bunch of baying Red Bone hounds.

After a long silence, Oscar said in a low voice, "Now that I have buried one of my children, I understand Mam and Pap and how they liked to never in time quit grieving over Elmer's dying so young and all. Elmer never was like the rest of us. It was like they could not figure out what to do with him. They grieved over his being so different, too. They never did figure him out, so they just finally just let him alone and allowed him to live at their house and do as he pleased. Now that he's gone it don't seem to matter what he did or didn't do, does it Tine?" Oscar spoke not expecting an answer from Tine.

She did not reply.

The air fell silent except for the occasional caw of a crow announcing to others that he had found a feed.

Tine pulled her sweater back up and put it on and buttoned it. The wind was beginning to get a bit nippy. Oscar moved over to Tine and gave her a habitual warm hug followed by a slow warm kiss for the day's visit's ending. He picked up his two big buckets of water. Tine picked up her two full buckets. They began their walks away from each other and toward their houses.

The autumn sun was beginning to head toward the West before it fell over the horizon behind the hills. They both had much work to get done before the day sank into darkness.

CHAPTER 9

Winter was harsh; spring came late; summer was in full swing. It was July.

Blackberries, as sweet as honey, were hanging in big pods and bursting with juice because the sun and the rain had been just right to grow the berries real big this year. Tine was sitting under the silver maples breaking beans. She longed for a blackberry pie. She closed her eyes remembering a berry picking trip she and the children took once.

Bentley agreed to allow Tine to use the boys for a day to do woman's work. He did keep Loy to help him on the produce run. Sylvie would have to help, too. She thought she was to grown up enough to help since she was planning on marrying soon. Sylvie hated the blue dye that dyed her hands and fingernails from the berry juice. Tine and Bentley both figured as long as Sylvie was at home, she needed to help. Tine was of the opinion that if you ate at a table, you should help work where you ate.

Susie would get tired and hot and whine before a day in the blackberry briars was over. Tine left Susie with Mam. Tine and the rest of the family tied coal oil rags around their wrists and ankles to ward off the chiggers. Tine put a big pair of Bentley's britches on under her dress tail to protect her legs, and so did Sylvie.

The children never did want to go berry picking. They hated it and voiced their discomforts at having to go out in the glaring sun in hot clothes and stay all day parting briars and tromping down weeds. Sometimes they got in a hornet's nest and got stung. It was an awful job, but berries were nature's bounty free for the taking.

Tine ignored their questions and comments. She needed the boys and Sylvie to help. They could pick fast and get into briars and into thick weeds and places where the berries were hard to get to and to reach better than she could, and Bentley would never help berry pick.

Eventually, Tine responded to them all in a calm even voice, "You all just have to shut up. I cannot pick enough berries to feed all of the family all winter long, so if you want jams and jellies for the biscuits this winter, you have to fall in and help me."

Tine picked up her garden hoe for a walking stick for a weapon against any surprised black snake that might alarm them hidden somewhere in the bushes of the berry patch.

"Why what is the matter with my big over-grown boys, almost men, wimpling out like a real sissy here. Blackberries sweet as honey are hanging in big pods busting with juice because the sun and the rain had been just right to grow them big this year. Blackberries are about the best thing in the world, and all a body had to do is go out and pick them is the message."

Tine loved the memory of berry picking days with the children. The crops were pretty much laid by when berry picking time came. Tine got a big kick out of remembering how much the boys hated to pick berries. They thought they were too big to have to pick blackberries as soon as they could plow.

Tine continued recanting the memory of the day she had taken them to the hainted house to pick the best berries she had seen that year. Tine recalled the whole day in detail. She could see Leonard and Ira and Sylvie and hear them, too.

Leonard said, "Mom, berry picking is work for women and children."

And Ira chimed, "I hate to berry pick. Can't I do something else?"

Tine grinned to herself about how she had gone about the business of getting ready to pick berries while totally ignoring Ira's protests.

She found an old pair of Bentley's work pants for herself and for Sylvie to wear under their dresses to keep from scratching their legs all to pieces on the blackberry briars. Sylvie returned from the lower room closet with two old men's shirts for her and Tine to wear to save their arms from being ripped up with briars. Their hands always just had to suffer the scratches and juice dyes. Sometimes it took a week for their hands to be white again after a day of berry picking.

"You all like blackberry jelly and jam on a piping hot biscuit from the oven with cow butter spread all over it. So, let's go. Those who like to eat have to work."

Tine made a paste of salt and lard to rub on the whelks if any chiggers did get on any of them. She always knew they all would be covered up with chiggers after a day in the weeds and bushes berry picking. She remembered how the children sat on the porch with their buckets. They sat with grimaces on their faces waiting for her to join them.

Tine had watched the briars all spring in that the old grown up front yard of the Ferguson house that had stood vacant for ten years. The place was all tied all tied up with heirs that wouldn't agree on what to do with the place. Tine was sad that the Ferguson's had let the place go like they had. They even went off and left some furniture in the house.

That last girl of hers that had the baby that nobody claimed took her woods colt, Tommy, and let out like a team of runaway mules when her mommy finally died. Nobody had ever heard tooth or toe nail of her since the day of the funeral. As best as anybody could tell, she must have hired somebody to take her and the child and leave.

Those other two girls come down from Ohio and Indiana in a truck and got what they wanted of their mommy's things and furniture. They loaded up the stuff they wanted and moved it to their homes. They left the rest of the whole place just like it was.

Tine had been in there just to spy around and see what was there four or five years ago before the yard got so grown up. There was an old piano in one corner of the living room. She did not touch a thing in the house, but she did pick her a vase of roses out in the yard to take up to the graveyard and put on Eunice's and Callie's graves. It wasn't stealing flowers if no one had lived there in forever.

First Ira, then Leonard, protested as Tine led her troop toward the old house when she turned down the dirt lane off the main road and did not offer to go into a field anywhere along the way.

"We are not going to that old vacant place to get them big berries in that front yard. Mom you know that place is hainted. Everybody knows that." They had sounded off to Tine in near unison.

"I am not afraid of ghosts," Sylvie noted. "I think they are just like angels watching over us."

Tine kept her eyes straight ahead. She knew that the best berries and the easiest ones to get were in that old front yard and garden. They needed to get their buckets filled before the summer sun got right straight up over them in the heat of the day. If each one of them could get their gallon lard buckets picked full really quick, then they could look somewhere else the next day for a new patch of ripened blackberries.

Once Bentley had told her that he and Oscar had been riding along there after dark coming home from going a coon hunting. Bentley said that he and Oscar both heard somebody throwing down lumber in that old barn up the hill behind the house. So, Oscar and Bentley turned their mules up the lane toward the house and road up to the barn.

When they got to the barn they hollered, "Is anyone there? Hey, who are you?"

Bentley said nobody ever did answer. So they turned around and started back down the dirt lane to the road, and they heard that lumber hitting the ground echo again, and both their mules spooked something awful and had come "a hair dab" running away with them in spite of all they could do. Both of their mules had never offered to run away before that night nor since.

Oscar also had told her the same story one day when they were talking. Tine had thought that even if Oscar and Bentley were right, no ghosts would bother them in a big group in broad open daylight. She had wanted the blackberries and she was going to get them.

Each one of the family worked concentrating as hard as he or she could filling their buckets. Large pine trees looped around the edges of the once yard and garden. They worked intently not saying very much. The quicker the buckets were filled, the quicker they could get away and out from here and get back to the house.

Every few minutes each one of the berry pickers would take a nervous glance up at the house. Curtains hung limp and dirty covering the windows. One of the front windows was broken. A curtain flopped up and down when a breeze stirred it in the broken window. The door stood wide open to the front porch. When winds shifted a bit, a loud creak echoed back in the house it seemed. There were no other sounds except of various unidentified birds in the distance calling to each other.

Yet, Tine and the children strained as if they were listening to something they couldn't quiet hear as they worked. When the buckets were almost finished and they had every berry off the briars, Tine instructed them. "Let's go around back to the garden."

The children did not protest. They knew Tine would not turn around and head for the house until the buckets were running over with berries. So, they followed her as she rounded the back porch that's roof had rotted and caved in on it. The back door was closed.

Tine parted the big weeds to the garden gate with her hoe and made a path for them to get to the berries that hung over the faded picket fence in big wads of ripeness. The old picket fence that separated the yard from the garden had faded from pure white washed white to an old dull gray. Some of the slats were broken and some purple and some white morning glory vines filtered up through the holes and ran along the slats or the jagged tops of the fence. The morning glories were all closed up in the noon sunlight.

They single-filed through the gate and each one headed for a different spot of thick briars to finish the day's picking. Tine went on toward the back of the garden towards the barn to finish her bucket. The barn had big old horse weeds higher than a man's head a growing right up to the open hallway. Vines covered the barn on all sides of it now. She was a little unsure of herself about getting that close to the barn because of Oscar's and Bentley's stories, but she shook off her uneasy nerves and went right on picking her berry patch clean.

She thought she heard music.

She stopped picking and listened. Chords rang out muffled-like, but she recognized the tune of "In the Sweet By and By". Well, Tine had thought, Aunt Matildy Allen must have gone up to the church to practice the piano to play the hymns for the summer revival that was to start this Sunday night. The children did not say a word but kept on picking.

Tine wondered if she were the only one who had heard the music. She shrugged the fearful feeling off and said to herself that the musical sound must have been the way the wind was blowing to carry the sound from over the ridge to here today. She picked on.

Then, she stopped and listened once more. She thought she heard piano music again. She set her bucket down this time. The sounds for sure were closer this time. She turned her head back towards the house. It seemed as if the music, this time, was from that direction.

She saw the boys leave their briar patch and inch in the direction of her and just picked an easy berry or two along the way. They looked at each other on those last notes she had heard and came in stepping unison right towards her real quick like.

When they got in ear shot of her, Ira questioned her in a tense voice, "Mom did you hear anything?"

Leonard followed his inquiry with, "Mom, we shore heard music, a piano being played somewhere. I know I heard somebody playing 'When We All Get to Heaven.'"

Tine remember trying to convince herself when she had answered, "I believe the air is a setting just right for us to hear Aunt Matildy Allen a up at Freedom Church practicing up to play the hymns for that revival coming here and stating this Sunday night."

Sylvie came ambling along with her bucket full. She said in a calm voice, "I heard music when I was close to the garden fence behind the house and I sung along with the music, 'How Beautiful Heaven Must Be'. I think there is angels in that old house a making music for us."

Ira said, "Sylvie, you are touched in the head. Mom says that is Aunt Matildy Allen practicing her piano over at the church across the ridge and the air is set jest right to carry it to us. How about that smarty pants?"

Leonard was uneasy. He said, "Let's all stand real quiet and listen and see if we all hear the same thing at the same time."

They all stood still and hushed up. All of a sudden loud as it could be piano music poured out from that old house. This time the music was not a hymn but an old Civil War tune. Tine recognized the melody of "Just before the Battle Mother".

With her hoe in one hand and her bucket in the other, even though the bucket was only half way, Tine let out as fast as her short legs would carry her. Right around the house she sped with the children right on her heels; they raced on the bent-over weed path and down the rutted lane to the dirt road. Sylvie was bringing up the rear. She stopped and looked back at the old house. The whole family scurried down the dirt road swinging their berry buckets. Berries bounced out of the buckets and onto the road leaving a blue-purple blackberry trail behind them. When they got to the main road, the rest of them hesitated in unison to catch their breaths and look back.

A woman's hand pulled back the curtain and held it back. Not a one of them spoke a word but jolted into a run like rabbits with a beagle dog on their heels.

As they got within seeing distance of their house, they slowed to a fast walk. Then they let out in a run down the hill the last few hundred yards back to their house. When they got inside the yard, they slumped down under the silver maple tree and slouched down under it each one sitting on a root that ran along the top of the ground.

After they caught their breaths, Tine implored, "Don't you all ever breathe that we heard a piano playing over there at that old house or we will never live it down."

Sylvie announced calmly, "I would like to get a better look at that woman that pulled the curtain back and watched us leave. She was all bluish white looking with beautiful long curly hair. There was a circle of some sort of pretty white light around her shoulders and head."

"Why, Sylvie, you are really touched in the head," Leonard had chided his sister, "You are seeing things."

"Well," Sylvie replied, "We all heard things, what's the difference?"

Tine was still.

Sometimes Sylvie's imagination worried her: it was so far-fetched. The boys looked puzzled. They did not speak about Sylvie's not being afraid of ghosts. They just had looked at each other in a frown at their sister's statements.

Tine broke the silence and said, "At least not a one of us spilled all of our blackberries, did we?"

They all just died laughing. Ira said, "Why I plum forgot about the berries I was scared so bad."

"Let's go in and I will make us a blackberry cobbler for supper. Your daddy will like that," Tine continued.

The girls headed for the vegetable garden to get the beans, tomatoes, and potatoes for Tine to cook for supper. The boys went over to the farm to feed the animals. They always tried to have the chores done and supper ready when Bentley got home from his long days out with his wagon and mules selling stuff off the farm to folks.

The family set down to eat. Everyone passed the bowls and dipped their plates full of all the good hot food and began to eat hungrily. No one said a word. Tine had prompted them not to tell about their all getting scared at the Ferguson house.

Bentley, all of a sudden, slammed down his fist because Susan was whining over her cornbread. She did not like the brown edges. He stood up and started to unbuckle his belt, and as he stood up he overturned the gallon glass jug of milk. The spilled milk splattered all over the table and sloshed over into the green bean bowl, the boiled new potatoes and into every other bowl on the table. A layer of spilled milk even stood on the top of the open jar of molasses and settled into a little still white pool like butter on a piece of half cold biscuit.

"Susan Marie, eat whatever your mother sets before you and dry it up right now, or I will give you five licks and send you off to bed with no supper," Bentley spouted out in a loud voice.

The other children sat silent and chewed slowly on their food with fearful eyes. They knew if they as much as made a sound, whichever one made the sound, he or she would get five licks or more. They did not offer any help or explanations. Tine started to protest, but she knew from the rushing blood and red of Bentley's face that the best thing for her to do was get out of his way. If she said any word, he would lunge into one of his temper fits and all the other children might get a hard, hard whipping with his belt before he give out and got a hold of himself.

Tine felt tears brim up in her eyes, and her chest was tight. She hated standing by and allowing him in his tantrums to beat on her children. She, in an abrupt turn, marched out the back door and let the screen slam behind her. She had never walked out and left him with the children. She knew she couldn't stop him. She wished to God she could stop him.

She marched right on out onto the dirt road and went as hard and fast as she could get going, traveling right down the middle of the road. She was mad enough to slap Bentley blind. She glanced back. Bentley was not following her. He was probably making the children clean up the mess that he had made with the spilled milk. The pan of pie on the back of the stove had escaped the spilled milk. Thank God for that.

Tine slowed her pace a bit and noticed the sun was beginning to set. She went right on walking. She went clean out of sight of the house and kept right on going past Bentley's and Mam and Pap's house. No one was on their front porch to invite her in or ask her any questions as to why she was heading down the road at supper time instead of being at home with Bentley and the children. Sometimes Tine despised having them be so nosey about everything she did.

When she got to the path that led from the road up to Oscar's barn, she turned and hastened her step towards his barn. She could hide out and calm herself down in his barn. Once inside the barn, she stopped to rest and to catch her breath. She leaned her arm up against the log wall of the barn with her head against it and with her face hidden in the triangle of her arm and elbow, she began to sob.

She couldn't take her children and go back home to her dad's. She couldn't take care of them all by herself either. They would starve without Bentley. Bentley would get all right in a little while and settle down to his old gentle self. Tine calmed herself with that thought.

She felt the presence of someone. Oscar rounded the corner of the barn into the hallway carrying a milk bucket in his right hand.

"Oh, God, Oscar," Tine whispered in a hoarse sobbing whisper. "I thought you would already be gone to the house to fix supper for your girls. I wouldn't have come here if I had a thought that you were still here. I am so sorry you had to catch me all tore up like this."

Oscar questioned in a matter-of-fact tone, "Did he hit you? Did he hit one of the children? I decided I would never hit my woman or beat up on my children when Pap used to hit on us all the time. Pap beat up on his animals, too. I never could stand to watch Pap when he flew into one of his beating spells. If a man is having a hard time with the crops and the hard work and things like that, I figure don't have a right whatsoever to beat up on any of his family or his mules or kick his dog or rooster or anything else.A man ought to keep a good study of his head and hold a steady hand, as far as I am concerned."

"We both need to go to our children," Tine offered. Tine abruptly shook her head to shed the memory of that day out of her mind.

CHAPTER 10

After the black berries were gone, Tine worked from daylight until the dark ushered her inside all the rest of the summer harvesting fruits and vegetables, then canning and drying the food for winter meals. August was filled up with just work and sleep.

A slow soaking, slow September rain was falling in gentle strokes like the trickles from a leaking bucket. Bentley was sitting half dozing in a chair in front of the fire place. He had one log on the fire to keep down a damp chill from the air. A hard fast knock sounded on the front door. Bentley thought to himself as he stirred to go towards the door, "Wonder who that could be at this time of day?"

Dark had already set in.

Bentley traipsed to the door and opened it peering onto the porch to find Tine's cousin, Frank.

Bentley spoke as soon as he opened the door, "Well, I do declare if it ain't Frank. Come in and take your coat off and take a night with us."

Frank replied to Bentley's invitation, "I don't have time to stay but I appreciate the offer. I am on my way over to Swamp Creek Bottom to get a young steer I bought off Old Man Chase Madden. I will have to stay all night with them. I will need to get a early start back in the morning. I am going to lead the steer back behind my mule. I hated to drop in on you all sudden like this, but they sent word by me to Tine. They wanted me to make sure Tine knew that her mommy is real bad and is asking for her. She keeps on calling out Tine's name. She got so bad a couple weeks ago she that she took to her bed and she ain't been up since. Carlista is there with her around the clock. Tine's daddy is not able to help much, you know. I swear to goodness I hate to bear this bad news. They don't think Tine's mommy will last much longer. She was the worst this morning she has ever been. She won't swallow even a thimble full of water. Carlista has to hold a wet rag on her lips and squeeze a few drops of water at a time into her mouth. They want Tine to come on tonight."

"I declare," Bentley sounded a sober response.

Then, Bentley reoffered the invitation, "Frank, I do wish you could stay with us. We'll feed you good in the morning before you leave. We even have some country ham."

Frank reiterated that he had to go on since the Madden's were expecting him. He waited just inside the front door to see Tine before he went on his way.

Bentley went into the lower room where Tine and the girls were finishing a quilt.

Tine came through the front door ahead of Bentley puzzled look on her face.

"Cousin Frank, how good it to see you," she said as he offered a firm hand shake; Tine held his hand. "Come in. Come in. Are you hungry? What are you doing over in these parts, anyway?" Tine implored.

"I hate to put it to you so fast like this, Tine, but, as I told Bentley, your mommy is real, real bad sick. They want you to come on tonight if you can. They don't think she'll last much longer. She has been calling out your name. Carlista said to tell you that she needs you to come and help her take care of your mommy."

Frank held onto her hand as he saw the fear appear in Tine's eyes.

"Lord how mercy," Tine breathed a prayer in fear.Her hands shook; then she lifted her apron and dabbed back tears. She swallowed hard.

"Mommy told me at Christmas that she was not doing good at all. She seemed awful weak and tired. I thought she just had had too much company and that she had got too tuckered out from cooking so much for all the children and grandchildren coming and going at Christmas time."

Bentley put his arm around Tine. The trio stood in silence on the porch. The rain tapped slow and seemingly sad little rhythms on its roof.

Frank dropped Tine's hand. He started down the porch steps. "I will be praying for your mommy and all of you, Tine. I have to be on my way so I can get on back to home tomorrow before noon. I will drop by your daddy's place on my way back home and check on you all."

Frank straddled his mule that sprinted on out the road on his journey in a single instant, it seemed.

Bentley spoke first, "You all get you quilting stuff put up as quick as you can. I am going out to Pap's and get you and Susie his best two saddle mares. You all get ready to go. You can take Johnny. You have to go on, Tine. The mares are easy. Susie can go in front of you and hold the lantern. You can hold Johnny in front of you. I will get Mam's side saddle for you so you can hold Johnny easier. I will get Mam to come out here in the middle of the day and cook dinner. We'll get by, Tine. You have to go to your mommy."

Tine shot him a grateful look and set out to get ready to go. She replied, "I'll get Johnny all wrapped up good so he won't get wet and chilled and catch a cold." She walked into the house and yelled at Susie, "Pack things, we are going to Mom's as quick as we can get ready."

Almost instantly, Susie entered the room with a pillow case of clothes for her, her Mom and Johnny. She handed a lit lantern to her father, "Don't forget to get us big saddle pockets. I will put this whole box of matches in my pocket so that they will stay dry in case the lantern was to go flicker out on us."

Bentley left the house with the lit lantern to light the short way out the muddy road to his father's house to borrow the mares.

Tine and Susie began to prepare for the ride into the night. Tine instructed Susie to go out to the smoke house and find two of Bentley's old hats for them to wear to help keep their heads dry.

"We will tie our heads up with head rags and then put Bentley's hats on over them. You will need to find us a couple of old top coats, too. We will need to put another big coat on," Tine said.

Tine's mind raced with anxiety and fear. They would not have sent Frank to bear them the news and ask for her to come if her mother were not close to death.

"I can't stand the thoughts of doing without my mommy," Tine thought, then she said, "Maybe this is just a little sick spell and mommy will get over it as soon as this weather lets up and the sun shines out right warm on her."

Bentley yelled from the road through the wet rain early dark, "I am back. Get yourselves ready and come over to the barn. I'll help you all get gone as soon as you can. Come on, hurry now. It'll be real late by the time you get there anyway."

Susie put on her big coat and wrapped her head up, then set her father's big hat on her head. Tine covered her head with a scarf and put one of Bentley's old felt hats on over the scarf. The hat brims would shelter their faces from the rain. Susie ran ahead with the filled pillow cases in hand. Tine went to the crib and picked up Johnny and wrapped him up real tight in the blanket. A large lump rose in her throat as she wrapped log cabin crib quilt around her son. Her mom had made that quilt for Ira when he was born. That baby quilt had lasted through all her children. The scraps of material had come from the cloth of home-made calico dresses.

Tine reached the barn hallway; Bentley and Susie had already filled the saddle pockets and Susie was in the saddle astride Old Mag. She had her lantern in hand ready to lead the way. She was intently listening to Bentley's commands.

"Hold your lantern up high. Old Mag will take you to Tine's home place. Give her her head. She knows the way." Bentley instructed twice.

Bentley held out his arms to take Johnny while Tine climbed into the side saddle. Once she was secure in the saddle, Bentley handed her the bundle with the child securely snug and asleep inside.

"Be careful. Don't let my boy get hurt. I couldn't do without him. I couldn't do without any one of my family," he supplied as he slapped Tine's mare on its rump.

Susie led. Tine followed keeping her eye on Susie's mare's tail. Susie and her stead would set the pace for the journey.

Bentley crossed the road and pushed up the foot path through the yard to the house to join the rest of his family. Bentley delivered from the darkness, "Tine, I hate that your mommy is so poorly. You might just have to give her up. You had better prepare yourself for that. All of us have to go sometime, just keep that in mind."

As the little procession anxiously pierced the night and as if to soothe all three of the travelers, Tine begin to hum, then to sing aloud to Johnny. She made up the tune and lyrics as she went.

"Little Baby Boy of mine, you just lie still; your mommy and your sister will soon have you safe inside your grandma's house. Sleep on, sleep on Little Boy, sleep on." Johnny did not stir under his blankets while being rocked by the rhythms of the mule's gait.

Mile after mile Susie and Tine sloshed through mud and water on the soggy night. They rode staying intent on the reigns of the mares. They did not speak except to give a low command such as "Easy" or "Walk" whenever the mares encountered deep slippery mud holes or ditches washed out by the rain that sometimes alternated between heavy downpours and a drizzle. Tine would lift her coat tail from time to time and place it over the baby to keep him extra dry during the downpours. She did not mind her damp stockings and wet dress.

She would soothe Johnny if he stirred a bit by saying, "It's okay, little boy of mine, we are going to see your granny. Be good. Be good, now."

As soon as Tine and her children entered her mom and dad's yard, her brother, Robert, ran to them and in words with a rush of words all tumbling over each other like the sounds of a flooded mountain stream, he ushered them inside with: "Tine, oh how glad I am that you are here. Mom is real bad. We sent for you, but we didn't know if you would come or not. Thank God you got the message. Let me take the mares to the barn. You all get in there by the fire. Get them wet clothes off. Johnny didn't get wet, did he? Dad won't go to bed. He is in the living room in a rocking chair just staring into the fire. Mom can't talk. Carlista is with Mom. Mom is bad, real bad."

"Lord how mercy," was the only utterance Tine made.

They entered the living room with the linoleum rug with its dark streaks. Footsteps over the years had worn the pattern off in places. The wooden floor under the rug had its imprint on it. Tine remembered the day her Mommy had gotten that rug. Pap had sold a big good calf and stopped by Mc Ray's Furniture Store on the way home and bought it for a Christmas gift. Tine could remember the joy on her mother's face at getting a real rug for the living room floor. Mom ran and jumped up and put both arms around her dad's neck. That was the only time Tine could ever remember seeing her mother hugging her daddy.

Tine spotted her daddy's shock of thick white hair above the back of the rocker up near the fireplace. He did not turn his head in their direction. He just kept on rocking and staring into the burning fire.

"Susie, take Johnny upstairs and lay down beside him until you are sure he is sound asleep." Tine instructed her in hushed tones, and then added, "Put him in behind you against the wall so he won't roll out of the bed. He should sleep through the night unless you disturb him getting him put down. If he whines, rock him. If he won't stop whining, come down and get me."

Susie tiptoed ever so lightly up the stairs as if she thought something would break if she set her feet down flat to walk.

Tine raised her hand to tap her father on the shoulder and arouse his attention, but, just as she raised her hand to touch him, Carlista burst into the room sobbing, "She is gone. She is gone! Oh God, she is gone!"

Tine grabbed Carlista and held her to her breast for several seconds while Carlista sobbed and groaned, "Oh, God, Mommy, Oh, God Mommy! Tine, it is over. It is all over."

Carlista began speaking in lurches. "Tine, I just couldn't get her to drink. The water drops I squeezed on her lips just ran off. All of a sudden, she just stopped breathing. I head the death gurgle! I knew it was all over."

Tine dropped her arms from holding onto her sister and went in a hurried walk down the hall into the bedroom where her mother lay. She fell to her knees and grasped her mother's still warm hand. She buried her face into the covers on her mother's body. Pains of grief shot through her head as if it would chisel her skull open and allow her head to hang onto her neck, and be left wiggling in two distinct parts.

"Oh, Momma, Momma, Momma," she belted out in hoarse whispers over and over again until she lost the sound of her voice. Her mouth was dry. No tears would come. Her chest felt as if it would explode into a million pieces; yet, it would not.

She thought, "I can't remember the last thing I said to her. All I can remember is that last time we visited her that she was holding Johnny a minute right before Bentley brought the wagon from the barn to take us back home. The last thing I saw my mommy do was to kiss Johnny behind his ear before she reached him up to me. I cannot remember the last thing we said to each other."

Tine rose from her knees. She lifted the sheet up over her mother's face and bent down and kissed the top of her hair. Slowly, as if an invisible weight was pulling her backwards, Tine plodded the short trip toward the living room where she could hear Carlista still wail in pain, "Oh, I do not want my mother to be gone."

Carlista was pounding the couch with her fists. Tine went to the couch and lifted her sister upright. She sat down beside her. Carlista began sobbing, and her tears flowed unchecked down to the front of her bib onto her apron lap. Tine swallowed hard. She moistened her mouth. She couldn't seem to swallow or speak. She just began to rub her sister's back in full circles of comfort. She stared blankly out in space as she stroked Carlista's back.

Their father spoke from his rocking chair jarring them alert. He did not stop rocking." Girls, I can't help you any. It is your momma's time to go and there is not one thing we can do about it."

Carlista fell still and silent.

Tine did not move or speak.

Their father in unison with his unbroken rhythmic rocking, in a sweet baritone and shaky voice began to hum an old hymn tune, "Farther along we'll know all about it. Farther along we'll understand why…" Then, he broke into full voice singing to his grieving children, "Cheer up my brothers live in the sunshine, we will understand it, all by and by." At the end of the song he changed into another mournful tune. His voice faded to silence. His rocking subsided.

Robert opened the front door. He took one look at his sisters sitting like rock statues staring into space. The hot blue blazes of the open fireplace shot angelic shadows on the wall.

In an even and calculated tone Robert questioned them; "She has left us, ain't she?" He went down the hall and entered his mother's bedroom quietly. He stood with his head bent and breathed softly the Lord's Prayer as if to offer comfort to someone else besides himself.

After he ended his prayer, Robert said to Tine, "You and Carlista hunt Mom's burial quilt. Dad already has her casket built. I will go to the barn and get it down from the loft; then, I will go on back home. I will be back in the morning real early."

He spoke to himself, "Pap won't last long without Mommy."

Tine spoke to Carlista and her father, "Let's go to bed and get some rest. We can lay Mommy out and wash and dress her in the morning. Dad, will you let me help you to your bed?"

"No, I want to go set by Grace until the sun rises. Just hand me my walking cane. You children, go on to be now. You'll need all your strength tomorrow," their father informed and instructed them in a weak but even voice.

Tine had stumbled through her days after her mother's death and funeral. She did not think she would ever enjoy herself again. She wished she still had Eunice to talk to. The loneliness was like a dark back pit deep inside her. October dragged by. November was slower. December came. December went. Christmas this year was not much to celebrate.

CHAPTER 11

After Christmas, winter days lagged by. It seemed to Tine that a day was a week's worth of time.

"Mom, can I please have a kissing party?" Susie questioned in a begging tone one night. "There won't be no church and not much school until spring breaks wide open. We need to do something fun. Mom can we please, oh please, have a kissing party while Pa is gone to Indiana to his cousin's funeral. He won't care anyway, not really. He won't be back on that bus until next week anyway. A whole bunch of us girls was talking at church about how we'd like to have a party. We are so tired of quilting and sewing and being in the house all winter, you know. Can we, Mom? Please, say yes," Susie pleaded. "I am so lonely since my sisters both married off, and now they never come to see us anymore. I hate it that Sylvie took her children, Cecil and Cecilia, off to Ohio. They just come home once in the summer. Sally has to cook Sunday dinners for all them old maid school teachers and their company. She can't get away to come unless there is nothing there for her to do over there. She has not been home a single time since Christmas. Mirara won't come to our house unless Ira just begs her to come. He always goes to her house to see her. I like her so much I want her to come see us."

Tine grinned. She had her back to Susie. She was glad to hear that Susie liked Ira's girl. Tine did too. Ira shore did take his time about marrying. Those two had been courting a long time now.

Tine could feel how still Susie's waiting in anticipation for her answer. Tine knew she was going to say that Susie could have a shin dig. In fact having a bunch of just about plum grown up young folks in always lifted her spirits. She loved to watch them cut eyes at each other and laugh and turn the radio way up loud, roll the rug back and dance. On occasion she liked to lift her dress tail and clog like she used to do at home when the radio was on and no one was watching.

Her daddy did not like dancing. Said it was the devil's work. Tine felt like dancing was letting some of the joy of living out. She didn't care what anyone thought about her dancing.

Actually, Bentley never danced with her, but sometimes if the radio was on and they were getting ready for bed, she would waltz around. When she ran and jumped into the bed after dancing around like that, Bentley always kissed her a good long wet good night kiss. After he kissed her and they rolled over to go to sleep, he'd reach over and pat her on the round of the butt. Tine liked him when he touched her without reaching for her private parts. She felt like he loved her then. She wondered how come Oscar understood her so much better than Bentley did. Bentley just didn't notice that she was a person, just a wife with things to do for the children and for him. Tine thought it seemed like no one noticed that she was a real person except Oscar.

"Please, Mom, pretty please," Susan was chiming into Tine's private thoughts.

"Yeah, you can," she answered Susan. There can't be no drinking. Don't invite a soul that might try to sneak some moonshine in. Your daddy would kill us if he found out there had been any drinking at his house. Things might get out of hand with no man here to put a stop to it."

Susie screamed with glee. And, then she ran to Tine and hugged her. She immediately made her a list of who she wanted to come.

68

"They is no reason to invite Mirara; she won't come with Ira gone with them to Knoxville and him not here," Susie figured out loud as she made her list to offer invitations.

"Mom will you make gingerbread and dried apple pies and sweet bread for us? Can we have coffee? Will we have plenty of milk, too?" Susie questioned her without waiting for an answer.

Tine laughed deep in her throat at the glee Susie was having over getting to have a party on Saturday night. "I'll tie in and make pull candy for you all. I will have time to do that all Saturday afternoon afore they get here. Don't invite more that about fifteen, or we won't have enough room to have real fun. Hurry now, get the mule saddled up and go around to the neighbors and invite the ones you want to come. You'd better include your cousins, or they will get mad at you. Don't leave a one of them out. Hurry on now and be back fore dark," Tine instructed Susie and ushered her on her way to folks to tell them to come.

Tine felt a surge of new energy. She had time to finish those new dresses for Susie and herself that she was saving for Decoration. The time to enjoy the dresses was now.

It was Saturday. Time for the kissing party was upon them. The kitchen was full of sweet aromas from the oven. The gingerbread's spicy aroma while cooling on the table penetrated the entire room. Susie turned her left hand up to the window light. The tiny diamond Elroy had given her for her fifteenth birthday gleamed. Elroy left several weeks ago on a bus for Fort Benning for training. He had just turned eighteen and the draft got him.

The draft was waiting for every man as soon as his magic birthday of eighteen came. The government did not waste a day a getting the draft notices out. Elroy got his on the third day after his eighteenth birthday. There was hardly a boy left around for any girl who was not already promised. Susie was proud she was promised to Elroy. Surely, the war would be over soon. Susie hated that old Hitler for causing all the trouble and the Japanese for bombing Pearl Harbor, too. It was not fair for the boys to have to go off to them old foreign places and fight.

At least, Leonard, her second oldest brother, did not have a wife when he had to leave. Magdalene from over two ridges away in the edge of Royal County was promised to him. The army was holding Leonard in the states in Texas on a base. Magdalene wrote to him every day. Every day the whole family hoped to goodness that Leonard could keep on peeling taters in Texas and not have to go be a ground solider in the heat of the battle like so many had to do.

Susie got so sad that she left the room if the radio had news on it or if the men or the women were gathered up a talking about it. She didn't mind praying at church for her brother and Wade Elroy, but that was as far as she wanted to think about it. She did not want to entertain any thought of going up on the hill to the cemetery and burying any body in her family or Wade Elroy. Surely, they would not die even if two of the Wilson boys had died in the war and them cousins in the same family. It was just too horrid to think about.

Susie patted her ring. She would just sit and watch everyone else have a good time tonight with the music and the kissing games (actually there really wasn't any kissing that happened unless some couple sweet on each other already snuck off and slipped a kiss in…they just called them kissing games cause the young people gathered up a hoping to find someone to kiss later, maybe).

They all would go crazy over pull candy. Nobody in the whole neighborhood ever had pull candy except at Christmas, if ever. Susie loved it because Tine had gone to such trouble for the party. She walked over to Tine who was still stirring up the last batch of gingerbread.

She gave her mom a swift hug and said, "Mom you are the best mom I could ever have. None of the other moms would think of a letting them have a party before spring breaks and warm weather comes."

Tine answered, "Did you ever think that I might be in need of a party to lift my spirits? I have not heard a word from Leonard in three weeks. I fear they may ship him overseas. No news is good news is what all the mothers say. Maybe we just need to celebrate that. I swear I have not done a single thing to have a good time in a long time. Maybe this war will end afore your Wade Elroy has to go across them waters. At least he is down in Georgia training for the time being. Be grateful that he is not sent to foreign soil like all the rest of these boys over eighteen around here in the neighborhood. I swear there are no young men around here anymore."

She slipped the last pan of batter into the oven and said, "Let's go get our finery on now and be back when this last pan comes out of the oven. We will be ready when the first one gets here. Let's try our best to look fit as a fiddle."

Two girl cousins, Osie and Vina, arrived first. They had bundled up against the wind with sweaters and head scarves and arrived just at dark. One by one they entered the house and untied their scarves and took off their sweaters and coats. All three of them were so excited that what they were saying tumbled over each other. Susie said in a loud voice, "Stop, one at a time please. One at a time, please. I can't tell a word any one of you all is saying."

"Lay your wraps on the lower room bed," Tine instructed them.

Vina had a little girl. Her daddy, Ance, was away in the war.

Vina spoke with glee, "Thank you all for getting me out of the house. The baby is weaned. She will be just fine with momma for a while."

Osie coming back into the living room from having laid her wraps across the bed announced to Susie, Tine, and the other girls, "I invited my cousin, Lester. I thought you all wouldn't mind an extra person coming to the party. His wife got burned up a few months ago. Early last spring when the weather got warm enough to do the wash outside. Lester built his wife a big fire to warm the clothes water black pot. Well, a big gust of wind came right out of nowhere like it does on March days, you know. Lester was in the barn working on mending the harness and he didn't see or hear a thing. That wind grabbed her dress tail and

Cynthia, that was her name, but he called her Cindy, started running like crazy toward the barn where Lester was. She was trying to get to him as fast as she could. Well, she was almost to the barn when Lester heard her screaming for him. When he rushed out of the barn and saw her coming toward him, her dress was already burned plum up and her petticoats had flames in them. He grabbed a saddle blanket and charged toward her with it as fast as he could."

"Lord, how mercy on him," Susie whimpered. "I bet he about lost his mind."

Osie stated, "Matter of fact, he didn't. He did the smartest thing on earth there was for him to do.He ran to her. He grabbed her by the waist. He wrapped that blanket clear around her and knocked her to the ground and with his arms around her rolled her over and over and over until the flames died down. Then, he laid there with her, him calling her name over and over and over. He slapped her face and everything trying to get her to talk to him. She never said a word. She was dead right then. Since they buried her, he just stays at the house and goes to the barn and feeds his animals; that's all he ever does. He stays all alone most of the time. Mommy, his sister, is the only one he talked to about it all. He comes to see us just every once in awhile. Last night he rode his mule over and had supper with us. I told him he ought to get out and come with us tonight."

He surprised us all when he said, "What time should I get there? Tell me exactly which house it is on Spring Lick Branch."

He actually chuckled a little when he said, "I'd hate for a widower man like me to knock on some woman's door looking for kissing party and it be the wrong house. Why a fellow might get shot doing such as that."

Tine and Susie reacted to Osie's story in unison, "Well, we are so glad he is coming. Maybe being here with us all will help him get over losing his woman in such a horrible way as being burned up right before his eyes!"

"There the rest of them are. There the rest of them are." Susie nearly yelled out in excitement.

"Vina in her calm voice said, "Someone get that radio tuned in and find us that good music. We can't dance without music, can we?"

Susie pulled back the edge of the curtain in the living room window to get a clear view of the boys getting down off their mules and horses and hitching them to the barn lot hitching post. She carefully evaluated the new one, Lester. She liked the way he walked. She wondered how come she never had seen him. He only lived about ten miles away. Looks like he would have been at a church revival or a funeral or something, she thought. She did remember Dad's telling them about some man trying to save his woman's life from a fire, but since she didn't know them, she had dismissed it as a sad story and thought nothing else about it. Susie kept her eye close on him as he plodded up the hill to the porch lagging a little behind the others fellows.

"It looks like there won't be much courting and certainly not a bit of kissing here tonight," Susie thought. "Everyone must have come to eat and dance. We will have great fun anyways," she thought.

She wished her Wade Elroy was here, then, she would have a dancing partner.

Tine offered greetings at the front door as the last guest knocked, "Come on in and make yourself at home everyone. You must be Lester; just throw your coats across that straight chair there. We are so glad you all come. Susie thought we could warm up the night air with some party time. Lester, how good it is to have you here. If you are Osie's cousin on her mother's side, you are most welcome. Come on in."

Lester held out his hand sort of halfway bashful with his eyes looking down part of the time as Osie introduced him to everyone there. Osie waited until last to introduce Susie. Susie held out her hand towards him. Lester looked up at her straight into the eyes.

"He has such wonderful starry blue eyes," she thought.

There was a deep dark sad look behind his eyes, sort of dull and flat, like that of a lost dog without any sense of a home.

For reasons she did not understand, Susie's fingers slightly trembled as he gripped her hand in a firm shake and said, "Thanks for having me, Susie. I had heard about you all before but had never had a chance to meet you all until now. It is my pleasure."

Susie moved away and started moving chairs so they could roll back the rug for the dancing that was about to commence. The boys helped roll the rug back. She listened intently. She liked to hear Lester say nice words to Tine like he did to her.

"Where in the world this sweet man has been all my life?" she asked herself.

A tremor ran right through her every time she glanced at him. Then, with a bit of guilt she thought of Wade Elroy when she glanced down at her ring.

"Oh, fiddle sticks," she thought. "Wade Elroy is gone, and I don't know if or when he will ever be back."

Susie slipped the engagement ring out off her hand and stuffed it as far down in the corner of her dress pocket as she could.She knew she wanted to dance with Lester. She knew she was going to do that no matter what any of the rest of them thought about her stepping out on Wade Elroy.

The cousins danced together and changed partners. Lester didn't dance much; he just sat in the corner chair and tapped his foot to them Grand Ole Opry tunes one after the other as the radio droned them out. Tine clapped her hands and patted her feet in time to the music.

Vina set out due to her Ance's being away fighting. Susie was glad she wasn't married yet. It was terrible to have to be so good like Vina while a man was away in an old war. At least, she was just engaged, not married, like Vina.

Tine called out about an hour into the dancing, "Let's all go into the kitchen and get us something good to eat. Susie, you come and cut the gingerbread for us."

Susie followed her mother into the kitchen, picked up a knife and began to cut the gingerbread into equal squares ready to serve.

"Take something of everything; there is a plenty to go around and for second helpings," Tine chimed out to the visitors.

Susie looked up as she slid a slice of gingerbread onto Lester's plate. They locked eyes and something unspeakable passed between them.

"I have always known him someway," Susie thought to herself.

Lester startled her when he said in a quiet voice so only she could hear him, "Can I come over to see you this Sunday evening about two o'clock?"

Susie dropped her hand down in the pocket that held the engagement ring from Wade Elroy. She pushed it down further.

"Yes, oh, yes you can. Why I would be delighted to have you come calling?" she heard herself answer.

Susie immediately thought, "My Lord, what have I done? I am engaged."

As everyone secured their wraps and left to go home, Lester hung back shyly looking down at the floor. Tine noticed that he seemed to want to talk to Susie alone because Lester was holding back from putting on his coat, so she dismissed herself to go to the kitchen and tidy up the place.

"Susie will see you to the door. Now, you come back and see us, you hear." She left Lester with that friendly open invitation.

Lester hung at the open doorway as Susie held onto the door knob to close behind him. "Susie," he asked quietly, "Do you know that I was married once, but I don't have no children. I ain't much, just a thirty-year-old single man, now."

Susie replied. "Yes. Osie told us about it. That don't make a bit of difference to me. You come right on Sunday. Pap will be back by then. Why don't you come for Sunday dinner and meet him, too?"

"I think I might know your daddy. I know that I know of him," Lester said. Then, he grinned as said, "See you Sunday, for dinner."

Susie shut the door and ran to the kitchen jumping up and down and saying fast as she could, "Mom, Mom, I can't marry Wade Elroy. I have to send this old ring back to him in the mail. Mom, Mom, listen to this. Lester is coming this Sunday for dinner. Dad won't mind, will he Mom? You think it will be okay with Dad? I just made a mistake a-taking that old ring. I was in a hurry to get married because all the boys were in the army getting killed or going away to get killed. I knew in my heart it wasn't right to promise him I would wait for him. Oh, Mom, will Wade Elroy forgive me, you think? Will God forgive me?"

Tine crossed the kitchen, pulled Susie to her and hugged in a big warm hug." Susie, you best follow your heart, child. You best follow your heart."

Tine lost track of the days, months and years after the deaths of her mother, Eunice and little Callie. She cried for months mostly when she was working alone. It was like the emotional insides of her had left like a rotting old log's. She felt like she was like a empty old log's outside casing just going through the motions of the endless work of keeping a home going. Susie went to help Mam every day because Mam just could not do her work alone anymore. Johnny's days at school left Tine alone while Bentley was gone from daylight to dark on the produce run. Her head hurt so badly most days that she had to stumble to a chair and sit until the intense pain subsided. Sometimes she wrapped a towel around her eyes to make the room dark in the day to help the headaches go away so she could resume her work. Seeing Oscar got farther and farther between. He had to stay home and keep his place going and Mam was no help to him anymore. Her trips to the well were less frequent and Oscar was never there when she did go to get fresh waster. Bentley went out to Mam and Pap's on Sunday afternoons and met up with Oscar there to visit and catch up on each other's goings and doings. She stayed home with Susie and Lester to keep them company while they were courtin'. People would stay bad stuff about them all if she left Susie alone with Lester afore they married. Johnny would always go off to the barn or corn crib and occupy himself. Sometimes she could lie down on Sunday afternoons a catch a bit of rest while Bentley was gone visiting.

Chapter 12

The winter was long. Spring came in slow. Oscar walked along the path towards the black gum well. It was a warm day in April, and his mouth and stomach felt as dry as parched corn. He needed a drink. He needed to see Tine and hold her again. He was so weak he couldn't finish the corn planting he had set out to do for the day. Oscar had just walked off and left his hoe lying in the corn patch. He would go back after the sun went down and finish his job. He sat down in the shade on the roots of a rambling white oak tree. He pulled his shirt tail up from down under his bibbed overalls. He yanked one side of the shirt tail out and wiped the sweat off his brow with the corner of his shirt tail; then, he climbed up on a boulder that had lodged in times past off to the side of the tree. Oscar lay back on the rock. In slow motion he unlatched the suspenders of his pants and let the bib fall down. He pulled off his shirt and rolled it up in a roll. He stuck the roll of shirt under his neck for a pillow. The shade-cooled rock surface felt cool to his back. He gazed up the hill towards the cemetery which he could not see through the thick leaves on the summer trees. He felt an instant impulse to go on up the hill and visit Eunice's and the baby's graves. He let the impulse die. He had to bury them both in his heart. Oscar pushed the grief down inside himself.

He swallowed hard, twice. "My wife and my child are just gone, gone." He spoke out loud as if someone were listening to him.

He wanted to see Tine. He wanted to talk to Tine. She was a well of comfort to him. Just sitting beside her and saying nothing always helped him feel as if things would always be for the best someway. Tine was not a complainer. One thing Bentley could never call her was a nagger of a woman. He and Eunice used to fight verbal battles and scream out at each other over nothing. After all their hateful bickering they'd go to bed and make love like two newly weds and forget whatever made them mad at each other. Oscar grinned at his memories.

Eunice never rubbed his neck and shoulders with warmth and tenderness like Tine did. Seems like it just come natural to Tine to know what to say or what not to say at exactly the right time. Tine was the only one who helped him a bit with his loosing Eunice and his little baby girl.

He wondered where Tine was and what she was doing today. Oscar turned over on his stomach. He put his elbows on the shirt and put his chin in his cupped hands. A chipmunk scurried out from under the rock where he lay and quickly disappeared under the next rock over from him.

Oscar laughed and chided him, "No need to be afraid of me little feller I would not touch a hair on you for nothing, boy."

He remembered all the times he and Eunice used to take to the woods and lie down in the leaves and watch the squirrels and chipmunks play. They would frolic and flirt and wind up making love right there on the ground with not a thing to cover them. It was a wonder somebody had not walked right up on them out there in the woods. Some hunter or some wanderer would a got his eyes full. Oscar smirked at the thought.

In an instant and abrupt outburst, Oscar started crying. He beat the rock with his fists until his knuckles bled. Then, he got up and lugged himself over to the big oak and started beating the side of the tree until the bark jumped off the tree under his bleeding knuckles.

While he was boxing the tree, Oscar screamed to the top of his lungs, "I hate you, God. I hate you for taking my woman and my baby girl away. You don't play fair. By God, you don't play fair. I can't live by myself. By God. I need Tine. I need Tine."

Oscar caught his breathe in a hoarse whisper, gasped out in lurching tones, "I can't have her. I can't have her. I can't have her. Damn it! Damn it! Damn it! Damn it anyway!" And finally in a low whisper Oscar breathed out, "Tine's my brother's wife, not mine. O, God, she is not mine."

Oscar subsided into sobs and quit beating the tree. He looked down at his oozing knuckles and sucked the blood off them. He spit the blood and salvia off in the distance. He sat down. He slowly put his shirt back on and lifted his bib and relatched the overall latches. He stared blankly down at his hands. The knuckles started to sting a bit. He rubbed them on his pant legs. He looked at the sun and decided he had better get on to the well, get a drink and head back to the cornfield. Mam would be calling him to supper in a short while. Oscar treaded on up the hill on the steep path to the black gum well. When he got to the spring, he knelt down on his knees in the damp moss beside the well drum. He cupped his hands full of the cool waters as they spilled over the edge of the dank black wooden log drum. He washed the stinging knuckles until they were painless. He washed his swollen eyes with handfuls of the refreshing liquid. Before he got up to leave, he drank and drank and drank one handful after another. He let the last gulps spill over and cool his heaving chest.

"I needed a drink from that black gum well spring real, real bad," Oscar wiped the rivulets of the water off his chin with the back of his right hand. He idled back down the path from the spring to finish his day's work.

CHAPTER 13

In August Arvella up and ran off from home. One evening when Oscar came to the house from the fields at supper time he found had found a note in the center of the kitchen table that read. "Gone on the bus to Ohio to get me a job. Be back when I have saved enough money to get a round trip ticket. Arvella."

Then, after a long winter up North, and her having written a letter a week to Oscar and Arleta, Arvella announced in a late June letter that Marjorie, her landlady, who had been "such a good friend to her", was planning on bringing her home in her nice big Buick car she had just bought new. (Actually it was almost new, slightly used, car; but, a real big nice one was the way Arvella wrote home about it.) Arvella reported in her letters that she and Margie went everywhere around town in it. Margie wanted to try the car out on a long time and meet Oscar and Arleta. Margie was "sure she would just love them from what Arvella had told her about them" was what Arvella had said in the letter.

Oscar didn't take much to Arvella's bringing a strange new woman to his house; but, he had Arleta to write Arvella back and tell her to come on home and to bring that woman friend of hers if she wanted; but, to make "shore that that Margie woman was not to expect any find doings down in the country at their house."

Oscar wanted to see Arvella even if she had left without a word ahead of time. He just wanted her to come home anyway she could. He didn't have the money to send her for a bus ticket round trip.

On the fourth of July weekend, Arvella and Marjorie arrived in the big car about dusk, Arleta squealed with joy and ran down the lane to meet them. She hugged and hugged Arvella and then clung to her sister's side every second. They had come to spend two weeks' vacation with Oscar and Arleta.

Oscar held his arms open and squeezed both his girls to his chest and lifted them off the front porch floor. They laughed with glee and giggled just as if they were his little girls all over again.

Marjorie just stood and watched. When Oscar let his girls back down, she merely, glanced at Marjorie as he held out his hand to welcome her and thank her for bringing Arvella home. He dismissed himself and went into the kitchen to continue cooking dinner for his girls and his guest. He missed Eunice.

He did not rightly know how to treat this new woman who had come from away from his holler for a visit.

After supper, the girls went down the path and out to Mam's so Arvella could visit with her grandma before dark.

"Come go with us, Margie," Arvella invited from the front yard gate.

Marjorie glanced down at her high heeled shoes and over towards the screen door to the front porch that entered into the house where Oscar was doing the dishes so the girls would not have to wash them after they got back from Mam and Pap's.

"You all just go ahead," Marjorie fired back to Arvella, "I will go in and help Oscar finish the dishes. Tell your grandmother I will get out there to meet her tomorrow."

Marjorie finished her cigarette, went into the kitchen and asked for an apron so she could help dry the dishes. Oscar found an apron in the trunk where he had left Eunice's things. He started to hand the apron to Marjorie. Instead of taking the apron from him, she backed up against Oscar close enough for him to tie the apron around her waist. Oscar was embarrassed but obliged Marjorie and tied the apron strings at her back. Oscar felt his body tremble when Marjorie stood close to him in the kitchen while he was trying her apron. They commenced to doing the dishes. Oscar could not think of a word to say to this city woman. He and Marjorie just washed and dried. She would look at him while he washed and she waited her turn to dry the dishes. Oscar thought he felt her brush her breasts against him once when she reached for a clean wet plate from his hands.

All at once Marjorie raved about how good his green beans were. "I swear, Oscar, I have never tasted anything as good as your green beans."

Oscar simply replied, "I will get out in the garden early in the morning and pick us another mess fir us then. We will have green beans again tomorrow night for supper."

"Now, don't you go to no extra trouble just for me," Marjorie trilled.

Oscar grinned a weak grin. "Picking beans won't trouble me none at all."

Arvella had made it perfectly clear in the letter before she got home for this visit that she was coming home for "just a short visit and not ever coming back home to stay." Oscar knew the real reason Arvella left home and ran away on that bus to Ohio was because she had not had much of a life since her mommy died. She had been a grown up little girl doing a woman's work with him no wife to help her. Arleta had cried her eyes out when Frances, over at the store, had told her that Arvella had run away up North on to find her a job. Arvella left word for Frances to tell Arleta that as soon as she worked out enough money and found a place to stay that she would send Arleta a bus ticket to come on up there, too.

Oscar did not know how he could live if Arleta left too; but, deep down he knew she was going to go just as soon as she could figure out a way how to go.

Marjorie set the table while Arleta, Oscar and Arvella finished up the supper. Arvella was a good hand to fry the ham. They all told her that while they were eating the evening meal.

The next night before Marjorie teased Oscar and told him that she needed a man who could act like a woman and cook and stuff since she worked at her telephone operator job all hours of the day and night. She went on and on about how good his country cooking was and what a good job he had done with his girls.

She kept saying over and over to Oscar. "Your girls are the best hardworking and good young ladies I have ever knew of and boy they surely can cook as good as anybody."

Every time Marjorie got a chance asked Oscar one question right after another about what type of jobs that he could do on the farm and stuff like that.

Oscar just answered the best he could.

Margie, as she asked to be called, insisted on going to the barn with Oscar to feed the stock and she laughed over the lambs. She squealed with glee when she held the baby chickens and they wiggled right out of her hands and flew to the ground to scamper under the comfort and protection of the hen's drooped out wings.

It had been a long time since a woman had been around the house and barn. Oscar found himself liking Margie's attention and having her being around. He noticed when she climbed the ladder to peek into the barn loft that Margie was a good looker. She had real good legs. Down in the barn hallway she leaned toward him and up at him with a gleam of invitation in her eye. He kissed her quick and good. Oscar surprised himself. After that kiss, she put her arms around him and asked him point blank.

"Oscar why don't you just throw some clothes in a bag, take Arleta and go home with me and Arvella. I can get you a good job real quick with all the skills you have used down on the farm. I know just the man who owns the grocery store right down the street that is looking for a good butcher."

Margie just swore that Mr. Polanski would like Oscar and hire him on as a meat cutter as much experience as he had had a slaughtering lambs, and pigs, and chickens and beef and stuff down on the farm like he had all his life. She even promised if he that if things did not work out between them that she would buy him and Arleta bus tickets back home.

"Oscar, you are much too young and good looking and gentlemanly to be stuck down in this old hollow farm hunkered down without a wife or any good paying job all your life." Marjorie chided him in a playful flirty voice.

Oscar had just stood there without saying a word. He was taking in ever word she said. He did not comment. He listened to Marjorie intently.

Even though a good long time had passed since Eunice and Callie's death, Oscar found that he could not sit still at night after the supper on the porch before dark. He would just start out walking almost every night. Tonight even though his girls and Margie were in the house, he was restless and began to pace; then, he headed out aimless in his journey. He moved from the porch to the yard. He found himself on the way to the barn. He felt drawn to the barn and walked inside the hallway. The mare mule, Jessie and her working partner, Jake, welcomed him with stomps toward their troughs thinking that it was feeding time. Oscar walked by each stall and spoke to them.

"We are not going out to plow in the middle of the night; Oscar just can't sleep—got a lot on his mind. Old Oscar's got a chance go get out of here and away from all the reminders of Eunice. I see her in the kitchen. I see her in the garden. I reach for her in the bed at night and she is never there. To make bad matters worse, at times I reach for Tine and she is never there, either. Sometimes when I go to bed, I wish I had Tine on my arm just like she is out there on that rock or in the mossy bed by the black gum well. I want Tine here to hold me like she did when Callie died. I want to hold her because Bentley don't. Tine can't be here. It seems that she keeps all tied up all the time now that the children are older. She can't slip away as often as she could when Johnny was a little baby and Susie had to stay and watch over him. It seems like the times I can get to see Tine alone seemed to have more spaces in between them. The only time I can be with that sweet and precious woman is when she can get away to the well or when she can get a little time to come down here; but, it is a rare time when nobody is around so we can be all by ourselves; so, we just have to do the best we can to help each other along, which is not good enough."

Oscar found himself chatting to the mules in a one way conversation that did not stop.

"I don't know if I can stand to leave you working buddies or not, he addressed the mules with gentleness in his tone. He stuck his hand through the feeding window and stroked Jessie's ears. She stood still while he did. Old girl, you and me been together a long time now. We work real good together, don't we, girl. The problem is I got an offer to go try to work with another girl, a city woman; but, I don't know if I want to do that or not. If ever I am going to get the nerve up to leave you all and Mam and Pap and Tine and Bentley, I ought to do it now. Arvella is already left and is all set up and if I don't take Arleta and go up there so she can be with her sister, the next thing I know, Arleta will be leaving me a message at the store that she has done gone on that bus to the North to be with her sister. She is about to turn into a woman early it seemed to him just like Arvella did. It is just a matter of time, don't you think, Jessie, that I will be here all by myself?"

The mule just stared at him with a blank look in her eye. She turned toward the wall away from him.

"I can see that you are staying out of this. Smart girl you are." Oscar teased the mule and himself with the statements.

Oscar found himself wanting to talk to Tine so bad he could hardly stand it. But, that was not possible to go to her in the middle of the night.

His mind turned from Tine to his mother.

Mam was plum worn out and did not need to be doing what she was doing for him and Arleta. Lord knows Mam had done enough in her day for all her children, especially since Eunice died. Mam did not need to have to be ready to help him all the time. Thank God Tine could handle all her stuff all by herself. She did not bother Mam hardly for a thing.

"Tine you are just one fine woman."

Oscar realized that he had spoken to Tine aloud as if she were present. He shook his head at his loneliness. "I may well be loosing my mind," he offered an apology to the stars.

He continued aloud, "Bentley, I swear, you do not know what a fine, fine, woman you married." Oscar added to the moon that was so clear bright that he could see his hand out in front of him.

He found himself headed up the foot path toward the black gum well. He knew every inch of the foot patch; he had no need of a lantern to light his way. He stopped and listened to a screech owl's haunting voice call from close by in the darkness. Oscar did not know what it would be like to go to town to live and leave the bob white calls and the morning glories. He never had lived without snow white frosts when wood smoke eased out of chimneys and perfumed the valley with that special left over scent that came from the warmth the wood let go of as it poured its heat into kitchen stoves and out of fireplaces in the houses of his family and neighbors. The smoke on a clear day always curled itself up to sky in a slow motion like it was spinning light bluish gray silk. He had not ever been over ten or fifteen miles from Pap's house and he never intended to live anywhere but right there next to Pap and Bentley. He just couldn't figure out what it would be like to live anywhere else than here at home.

Oscar reached the ravine that secured the black gun well. He found his way up onto the rock in the darkness. The water made a sound like some sort of angelic harp music trickling over the sides and down the overflow stream down the hill. Oscar laid back and stared at the stars. He crossed his hands under his head and cupped it to cushion from the surface of the rock. He let the memory of Tine and her gentle voice and soft comforting loving hands run over his body and his mind savored each inch of memory as if the memories were now instead of then. He could hear her soft whispers of love and reassurances in his head. Oscar gazed at the darkness where the grave at the top of the hill held his bride and best friend. He wondered if Eunice could talk what she would say to him.

She probably would make a joke and say, "Oscar, you are a country boy, and you are not cut out to be with no city girl. You could well bite off more than you can chew. Now just think on it."

"Well, I am thinking on it," Oscar answered his imagined reply from Eunice.

That woman, Marjorie, that wanted to be called Margie, was a good looker. She had a job. She did not want children and said there was a way to keep from it that she would show him. She had punched him in the ribs and said something about that they would visit the drugstore and get fixed up. Well, there was whole bunch of them city ways he had to learn; but, she promised to teach him. She had said her house could be his house and the girls would always be welcome there. She also knew she could get him a job. Oscar's head was spinning with thinking about this new woman Arvella had brought home with her.

"The same road that goes up there comes back," Oscar thought. His mind went on to thinking about how Arvella had made it good and clear that she did not want to ever come back to that holler; there were just too many bad memories since her mommy died in that house.

Oscar had a mind that Arvella was right about that. He could hear Arleta cry sometimes deep in the night, still. Maybe if Arleta could get in town with her sister, she might get over her mommy's being gone and her sister going off like she did. Oscar hated that Arleta was so hurt and lonely. He felt helpless when he tried to offer her comfort; so he just went off and let her cry all by herself most of the time.

Somewhere in the distant on the top of a ridge a coyote called shrill and wicked sounding. Oscar hated them varmints. He hoped they would not bother his new heifer calf in the north field away back from the house. He sat up. His back hurt. He wished he had Tine with him.

She would rub his back. He slipped off the rock and inched toward the well. He bent down and sucked a good long drink of that sweet water and sloshed it around in his mouth before he let it slid gently and easily down his throat. That water was as sweet as the kisses he got from Tine. Oscar looked toward Bentley's house but couldn't see it for the trees. He turned and inched his way back down the hill and around the back of Mam and Pap's garden and on back past the barn to his house. He crawled back into his bed without pulling his britches off. He went to sleep. He dreamed he was sleeping on the mossy bed beside of the black gun well and soft pine needles fell on his face like feathers tickling his face.

Oscar awoke from the dream, got up out of bed and went out on the porch; he couldn't sleep a wink. The moon was shinning as bright as daylight. He listened to screech owls in the limbs of the maple trees he planted before he and Eunice married. He had staked out a lot off Pap's land to build him a house when he was about fourteen. He thought that this place would his home his whole life. Eunice took to the place the very first time she came to visit. That was a big reason he married her because she was so satisfied here.

Oscar blushed a bit. The first baby that was stillborn was born just seven months after they were married. It had not mattered to him if the folks around gossiped about the quick baby they had. It was his business if he and Eunice made love before they were married. He never had apologized to anybody about Eunice's being in the family way already on their wedding day.

Oscar put on his work shoes without and socks. He didn't even bother to tie his shoes. He let out walking. He did not know where he was going. He just had to walk. He walked out the road toward Bentley's. He wanted to go to Tine. He knew he couldn't.

He turned and started up the path where he always found her on hot summer evenings when she came to get water and rest a spell in the heat of the day.

Tine had never offered to come stay with him. He had never asked her to do that. He wanted her but there was no way they could be together, unless they just run off and left her children and he left Arleta. Mam and Pap would be left to take care of the children.

Oscar knew that he would never ask Tine to leave her children, even if he could ask her to leave Bentley. Oscar sat on the rock beside the spring staring into space for the longest time before he got up and treaded back down the steep path. The moon was sinking out of sight. Soon it would be dawn. Oscar did not need a light. He knew each inch of the trail.

After he got back to his house, he slipped back under the covers of his bed with his clothes on; but, he never closed his eyes for one wink of sleep.

As soon as it got daylight, he got up and punched up a fire in the cook stove to get the stove heated up to cook breakfast for his new family.

CHAPTER 14

That night Bentley came in through the kitchen door and hung his hat on the wooden peg beside the door. He ambled toward the kitchen table, pulled out a chair and sat down as if he were in a stupor. Tine turned from the stove where she was stirring a pot of pork ribs and potatoes that were nearly finishing cooking for supper. Bentley usually went into the living room and waited until she called for her call to come to the kitchen and eat. Tine looked at her with a questioning glance. Bentley was home earlier than usual. It was best to stay out of a man's business. She dared not to ask him questions.

Bentley always got irritated if he was asked to tell why he was early or late a coming home. Tine crossed the kitchen to the cabinet and took out the plates to set the table. She put the stack of plates on the corner of the table.

Bentley moved his arms to make room for her to set the table; then, he spoke to Tine in a tone that sounded as if he were as addled by being hit over the head with a falling tree limb. "You will never believe this. I stopped by to check on Mam and Pap on my way in. Mam has been crying all day long."

Tine stood still and waited for him to go on. She knew that something was terribly wrong. She dared not interrupt Bentley in the middle of his story. If she did interrupt him, he would fly off the handle. She let him have his good easy time to relate whatever had happened.

Bentley continued without a look a Tine. "Oscar up and left with that woman, Marjorie, that Arvella lives with. He took Arleta with them. They just gathered up their clothes and locked the door and left. I reckon Arleta wanted to go live with Arvella. So, that woman talked Oscar into going with her. I reckon he is going to marry her according to what he told Mam and Pap."

Tine gasped. She threw Bentley a look to see if he noticed her reaction. He was so deep into thinking about Oscar's leaving them all, he would not have noticed if the house was a fire.

Bentley continued shaking his head in disbelief, "Get this, Oscar told Pap to just take as many of the animals that he wanted and to give me the rest of them or all of them. He said that to just let the cattle stay on his farm and for me to go out there and feed and take care of them. He wants to keep the farm and the house. I can't believe this out of him to save my life," Bentley spouted out. "Seems to me like Oscar is grasping at straws trying to get a new instant family by going up there to that woman's house and starting over without knowing what he is getting into. Since Arvella got herself that bus ticket with the money she had saved up from selling blackberries, plus her writing that cold check on Pap to get her enough money to go get her a one-way ticket on a bus to hunt her good job in the city, Oscar just got worse and worse off. I reckon Oscar has about grieved himself to death since Eunice died. There don't seem to be a woman around here anywhere that is a bit interested him. I know he told me that he did not want to marry a woman with a bunch of children to raise. Around here, if there is a single woman, she is widowed with a bunch of children."

Tine clutched the plate and did not put it down. If she turned loose of the plate, she knew her hands would shake. A stream of that hot black pain hit her on the right side of her face above her ear. She took the free hand and held it above her pain filled eye and closed her eyes until the pain subsided.

Bentley did not notice her grimace. Tine stood frozen in her tracks. She could barely stand to listen to Bentley; but, she had to know it all.

Bentley continued, "Mam just a kept going over and over saying the same thing. 'Why, he doesn't even know that woman. No good will ever come from this. Oscar has lost his mind.' Pap was taking it all in his stride. He kept saying to Mam that Oscar was a grown man and that there ain't a thing they could do but let him go. Pap also told Mam that a man needed a woman to help him with two girls that were almost grown women. Pap reminded Mam that those girls and Oscar had been without a mom and wife for a long time now. Maybe it was time for Oscar to make some sort of a change."

Tine's eyes cleared and the pain in her head just dropped to her heart. Her internal self was screaming in her ears, "He had me. He had me. I couldn't go live with him and Bentley being his brother. I couldn't take my children and leave Bentley. Bentley would have a killed us both. Mam and Pap would not allow me to ever set a foot in their house again if I left Bentley and took Oscar."

Tine felt as if her guts were rolling up in her throat. She almost gagged aloud. Her mouth was dry. She could not speak a word. Thank God Bentley did not look at her now. She finally was able to set the plate down. She put both hands on the back of the four-posted bark-bottomed chair to steady herself gripping the chair back so hard that her knuckles were all blue. She could barely hear what Bentley was saying. He sounded like he was far away. Bentley's voice was hollow to her as Tine tried to grasp the reality that Oscar was gone, really gone.

Tine's head was shouting to her. "Get out of the house. Get out of the house. Get away from Bentley. Go now!"

Bentley continued, as if he were talking to himself, "I have never lived without Oscar around. I can't remember being alive without him. He was my bed feller until we left home and got married. We are always helping one another. Before we married, he was the one who got the idea to hollow that black gum tree out and set it at the spring to make a well drum that would always give all of us water when we needed it. He thought that if him and Eunice or Mam and Pap needed water either, that there would always be water for all of us there."

At Bentley's mentioning of the black gum well, Tine rushed over to the water bucket and grabbed it. The bucket was not empty. She did not care. She had to have a reason to leave the house. She did not speak. She pushed the screen door open without a word. She ran-walked across the yard, through the barnyard, across the wooden foot bridge, and up the cow path to the black drum well. When she reached the spring, she slung the water bucket toward the black gum well with all her power. She wished that Oscar was here; she would have lashed him good with that water bucket for not telling her one word ever that he wanted to leave. The only thing he had ever said was that he shore did hate that Arvella had run off and left him and Arleta. He said that he guessed Arvella was tired of being a momma to Arleta and doing stuff around the house a wife ought to do instead of a young girl; but he never, ever, not even once even hinted that he wanted to get away himself.

Tine fell to her knees face down into the moss that blanketed the earth around the black drum well. She buried her face deep into the softness of the moss, much like she had buried her face into the softness of Oscar's shoulder. The dank earth's aroma penetrated her nostrils like some ancient balm to still her shaking being. Her breath eased from her rushed run-walk to the ravine where the black drum spring had awaited her. The sides of the ravine wrapped around her and held her close. As soon as her breath eased, she began to groan. She dug her fingers deep into the moss as if to try to find some evidence that there was something left of Oscar to hang on to…but the black soil did not hold him. He was gone. Her entire body writhed in pain like a black snake's body held by someone trying to kill it under a sharp hoe with its head half already cut off, not yet dead and not yet fully alive. She could not think. She could only allow the pain of separation tear at the muscle tissues of her body. When her writhing subsided, the pain gathered in the deep tissue of her heart and settled like a permanent knot of tightness in her chest. She struggled to breathe. Then she began to gasp out hoarse whispers, "I don't know how I can stand it without him." She whispered the hoarse words until she had no sounds to utter.

She wallowed on the cushioned moss bed until she could no longer move. She just lay with still her muscles aching and limp. She tried to pray; but, prayer stuck in her throat. She remembered that the Bible had some sort of verse that Jesus was already praying for you when you could not pray for yourself. She hoped Jesus was praying for her now because she certainly couldn't pray for herself. She found she could not pray for Oscar either. Tine did not ask God to bring him back because Oscar left on his own.

As Tine turned over on her back and looked up, dusk was beginning to drift in. The pine tree shades grew heavy and thick. She remembered that there was food on the stove about ready to eat. There was no bread in the oven. If the children did get hungry before she got back to the house, they wouldn't starve. There was food warm in kettles on the stove. Both she and Mam had always waited on Bentley "hand and foot" so he probably would wait to have her fill up his plate for him before he would eat.

Anger welled up inside her and she kicked the moss. She kicked into the moss until her toes ached from being jammed against the rocks underneath the moss. Tine dragged her dry-eyed self up to the edge of the black gum well and let the spring's stream of cool water fill her cupped hands. She sloshed the water all over her face. She held little hand cupfuls over her eye lids to take the cry swelling out of them. She hoped her eyes would not be red when she got back to the house. She cupped her hands and sucked up a couple of scoops of water from them. The cooling water refreshed her aching throat. She set herself down on the rock where she and Oscar had held each other. One tear slipped down and off her face to her shoulder.

She could up and leave just like Oscar did. Then, Tine reminded herself that she could barely go at times especially after them awful headaches and dizzy spells. There was nowhere to go. A woman couldn't go away and find work if she had children. No other man would take her if a woman had children. Lord, knows she did not want any other man's children to raise. She was glad that Bentley had made it so that she would never be in the family way again by staying away from her and not ever being in the bed with her under the covers. If she stayed put with Bentley she would never have another baby.

Dusk was changing to dark fast.

Tine had to go back to the house. She pulled herself up from the ground. She mustered up enough strength to begin her weary steps back down the path toward the house. When she got to the foot log, she could hear the mules crunching corn in their troughs in the barn. She knew then that Bentley had gone to the barn to do the feeding. She hoped he had not noticed how long she had been gone after a bucket of water and supper not ready. She hurried her steps towards the house. When she entered the back door, she set the water bucket down beside the other bucket. The children were all at their plates eating ribs and potatoes without any cornbread.

They stopped chewing and looked at her with puzzled expressions.

"I was so tired that I had to rest when I was at the spring," Tine offered an excuse for having been gone so long.

Susie spoke, "Daddy told us to go ahead and eat if we was hungry that he would eat after he got the feeding done. Daddy said to tell you that after he got through feeding the stock here at the house that he would have to go out to Pap and Mam's and help Pap get Oscar's animals fed. Daddy told us that he had already told you, Mom. What do you think about Uncle Oscar's running off real quick like that?" Without waiting for an answer Susie continued, "Daddy said to save him his supper and he would eat when he got back to the house."

Tine found enough courage to try to speak and answered Susie in a level, but firm voice that surprised herself, "Uncle Oscar is your Daddy's best friend in addition to being his brother. We will all miss him and Arleta."

The children finished their meal in silence.

Tine dismissed her children from the kitchen with these words, "Go on, I will do the dishes by myself tonight."

After that night, Tine went though days and weeks without thinking or feeling; she simply was just going about the work that had to be done. She fell asleep exhausted at the end of everyday.

She would not think on Oscar.

CHAPTER 15

It was late August and nearing Labor Day and time for the Sylvie and her family to come home for a week.

Sylvie, Tine and Bentley's second child and her man, Jonah, had left their little patch of ground, tiny farm, where they had lived since they married and their two children were born to go look for work about five years ago. The children, Cecilia and Cecil, were four and five years old they took them away to start school in the city. It was. Jonah could only have one week a year in the summer off from his job at the zoo where he worked keeping the zoo stalls clean. Jonah said it was cleaning out the barn except the manure was from all kinds of animals from around the world instead of from horses, mules and cows.

Sylvie was so fond of Pap and Mam that she went to their house first for a night or two before coming on home for the rest of the week with Tine and Bentley. Today the grand children were out at their great grandma and grandpa's house playing in the swings Pap had made for them under his big oak tree in the front yard there.

Cecile and Cecilia, Sylvie and Jonah's two children, always cried when it come time for them to leave and go back home. Tine cried, too, when they left; but, not until they were plum out of sight. She did not want the children or Sylvie to know how badly it hurt her to not be able to see them but once a year.

Jonah was over at the barn lot helping Bentley work on repairing harness. They had found a cool spot to work in the shade of a big old black walnut tree.

Tine and Sylvie were in the kitchen preparing dinner for the men.

Tine handed Sylvie the peeled potatoes to rise before she transferred them into the pot of hot water already in the iron pot on the back of the stove. The late July humidity had all ready set in even though it was only ten o'clock in the morning. Jar flies whistled their low monotonous warning that summer in the southern mountains was in full swing. Sweat poured down Tine's backbone and down between her breasts. She lifted her apron tail and wiped the perspiration drops off her forehead and upper lip. She dumped the peeled potatoes into the hot water. She added a pinch of salt and placed the lid on the pot.

She turned to Sylvie and said, "Go to the cellar and get two jars of sweet pickles, and two jars of them dill pickles, too. I will cut the ham and start frying it. I will add water to the left over green beans. There is a plenty of them to do for our dinner."

Sylvie did not respond. She just stood still. Sylvie was looking out the back window over the kitchen sink. She squinted her eyes as if she were trying to see something far away. She stood frozen. She concentrated so hard that it seemed that she was the only person in the room.

Tine noticed her still quiet stare and hesitated as she added more wood to the side of the wood stove. She slowly closed the door on the fire as she intently watched Sylvie to see if this staring spell was for just an instant; or, to see if Sylvie were going to go into a trance like she had been doing fairly often lately. Tine swallowed hard and caught her breath as Sylvie started out saying foolish sounding stuff.

Sylvie barely whispered, "There she is Momma. Watch her. She is coming right down the hill along the rail fence. She is just a floating a long. She is so beautiful. There she is smiling at me." Sylvie sounded as if she were a child cherishing her new Christmas doll. "Ohhhhhh, she is a waving at me now. She just disappeared behind the smoke house. There she is again. Oh, Momma, she stuck her head back around the corner and waved at me. She isn't a going to stop and talk to me today. Sometimes she does though." Sylvie clapped her hands with glee. "Oh, there she goes; she is a flapping her wings to get ready to go. She is sooooo beautiful with a trailing pretty light blue gown today. There she goes, Momma. She barely tip-toed across the top of the pear tree and she is a drifting up to the clouds. Sometimes she stays awhile and talks to me. If she comes about my bedtime, she sits on the side of my bed and talks to me."

Tine interrupted her. "Sylvie, Sylvie, snap out of it. You are sounding out of your head. Don't you tell anybody else that you are seeing and a talking to angels! They will call you plum crazy. You are going to keep right on until you go completely right off your rocker."

Tine frowned as she turned the country ham over to brown both sides equally in her big iron skillet. She could not understand these spells that kept coming over Sylvie where Sylvie just swore she was seeing things and talking to people that were not even there.

"You need to get your head straightened out, child," She chided her grown-up daughter.

Sylvie did not respond. She stood gazing up the hill where she had seen the angel ease out of sight into the high clear sky. She lingered a few seconds, then, turned to her mother.

"She has picked me out real special. She told me the other night that I am the only one she allows to see her and talk to her. She told me that she only come to the one who believes that she is real. She knows that I believe. She even told me her secret name, which I ain't allowed to tell anyone. She has a special name for me too; but, I can't tell a soul, not even you, Momma; because if I do, she might not ever, ever come back to see me." Sylvie sounded as if she were a child instead of a grown woman as she narrated her story to Tine.

Tine's chest tightened. She did not know for the life of her what in the world had got into her child lately. She always had good sense until her and her man, Jonah, went off to the city where they lived amongst all those queer people from all over the world. Some of the children that were their neighbors couldn't even talk in English. There was a ton of them folks from just about everywhere in the world. They did not have a yard or a garden. Sylvie was stuck all day long with nothing to do in them four walls while the children and her man were gone out to school and work. There was a place not in the world for her to even go out for a walk outside. Whores and drunks came out on the streets at night and kept them awake under their bedroom windows. At least that's what Cecilia had told Tine. Cecilia was big enough to know what the truth was going on around her. When Sylvie weren't around, Cecilia and Cecil would drop her enough details that Tine had figured out what kind of conditions they lived in. Tine knew she would loose her own mind if she didn't have her birds and her flowers. It was nearly time for the fall crop of wildflowers. She had noticed a deep purple iron weed that had bloomed early down in the meadow when she went after Old Jers to come down to the milk gap the other day. She loved the fall wildflowers the best. It seemed to Tine that the colors were the brightest right before the end of the summer and the beginning of the fall. Golden rod was about to burst open in yellow, too. Purple and yellow were the prettiest colors in the whole world.

"Nature just makes a giant flower garden quilt for us," Tine reasoned to herself.

She wished Sylvie had pretty stuff to look at instead of them old dirty city streets out her windows. Five years up there had sure put her head in some sort of foolish spin.

"Maybe this crazy stuff with Sylvie will pass," Tine tried to self reassure.

Bentley had said for her to not pay any attention to Sylvie's foolish talk and it would go away. But, Tine couldn't keep her mouth shut when

Sylvie got too carried away with telling about seeing things nobody else could and talking to people that did not exist. That scared the living daylights out of Tine. She had heard of stuff like Sylvie was doing but never around close or in the family like this. Tine instructed Sylvie to watch the stove while she went to the well in the side yard to draw a bucket of water. Tine used this well very sparingly because it filled back up slow. She only used it when she did not have time to go to the black gum well.

As Tine crossed the yard, she wondered what in the world was happening to all the family that went up North to work. As soon as they got to the city, they started changing getting real queer ideas. Like she could not understand how on earth that Oscar's Arvella ever got connected and mixed with that Marjorie that Oscar left with in the middle of the night.

Her chest tightened.

It was not fair any way you looked at it for that woman to come down here with Arlene and carry on like she did when everybody knew that she was just looking for a man. Tine hated her with her bleached hair and red lipstick and painted red fingernails. She came down here with only her high heeled shoes to wear in this mud and dirt on the outside. Mam said that the way she got in with Oscar was that she went to the outdoor toilet in them crazy shoes and they mired up over the spiked heels. And, that Oscar went down towards the toilet and picked her up and carried her back to the house so she would not mess up her shoes in the mud. She wore them fancy clothes and did not turn her hand to help Oscar's girls do a thing while she was visiting them that first time. Arvella said that Marjorie offered to bring her down for free in her car so Arvella would not have to ride the bus. But, Mam said that Marjorie's real reason for coming home with Arvella was to meet Oscar. She was on the make or she would not have taken up with him and a loaded up Arleta and him to go back to her house. Truth is that woman already had boarded Arvella and knew what a good worker she was.

Marjorie knew that Arvella had even saved from berry picking that half-way got her a bus ticket to go up north to the city to get her a job. Marjorie knew from Arvella that Arleta was doing the cooking and cleaning and the garden work and everything for Oscar. She knew that Arleta was as good around the house as Arvella was and that Arleta could and would work just like Arvella did. After Eunice died and left the girls at such an early age, they both could do about anything a woman could around the house. Tine knew that she and Mam had taught Oscar's girls real good how to carry on without a mother. Oscar knew that, too. It made Tine so mad that she could bite nails in two pieces to think that Oscar took Arleta up there to keep house for his new wife. He suckered in with her like David done with Bathsheba in the Bible. He hauled off and a married her just as soon as Arvella introduced him to that man at the big grocery store that gave Oscar a job. That man hired Oscar as a butcher just as soon as he had seen how good Oscar already was at cutting meat.

It just didn't seem right some way for Oscar to be gone with a strange wife and taking his girls away from Mam and Pap and all of them like he had.

As Tine pulled the well rope up with extra strong jerks, she silently cursed at Oscar. "Why in the name of God had he took mercy on that woman and helped her wash her clothes when she fell on the muddy bank trying to cross the creek over to the chicken lot?" The girls told Mam that Oscar had gotten her one of Eunice's gowns and then wrapped her up in a quilt while he heated water and washed that muddy dress. He even cleaned the mud off of her shoes, too. Tine spit out salvia like a man at the thought of Oscar's cleaning up Marjorie's spike heeled shoes.

Best they could tell, the girls told Mam, Marjorie was kissing on Oscar in the kitchen as soon as her dress was drying behind the stove. By the next night, they just loaded up their clothes and stopped to tell Mam and Pap that they were leaving.

"I could have killed Oscar for that for not telling me and Bentley that he was going away," Tine hissed her anger out.

Oscar had not written back one line to them. His girls wrote to Mam and that was all the news there ever was about him.

Oscar and Marjorie just did not come home. Occasionally the girls would come to Mam's at Decoration; but, they didn't offer to come to her house and stay all night.

Susie and Johnny always had work to do; so, they did not go out to Mam's to visit them except for a few minutes after supper about once or twice while they were at Mam's. Susie said they did not talk about anything except to brag on their running water and indoor toilet and gas cooking stove. Arleta had quit school, too. Arleta was just to keep the house clean for Marjorie because Marjorie had a job as a telephone operator. Mam said that Marjorie won't wash dishes because it messes up her red polished nails; so, that's what Arvella told Mam. Tine was sick to her stomach when she heard the news from Mam about Oscar and his family up North. Oscar could have his citified woman and his citified ways.

It was like Oscar had died only harder for Tine to bear her grief because he was alive and she could not see him, or talk to him, or touch him.

Tine entered the kitchen and set the bucket down.

Sylvie had set the table and volunteered, "I'll go get Dad and Jonah, Mom, while you get the bowls on the table and the glasses filled. Jonah will want water. I want a glass of milk. That milk we get in the city just ain't as good as the milk Old Jers puts out for you all."

Jonah and Bentley hung their hats up on the corners of the doors. They all sat down to their food.

Bentley bowed his head and began the blessing of the food, "Dear Lord, thank you for this food and for the hands that prepared it...."

As he was praying, Tine peeped out of the corner of her eye that she was shielding with her prayer hand. She watched Sylvie who had not

105

bowed her head for the noonday blessing. Sylvie leaned over to towards the kitchen window and smiled and smiled then waved and waved.

At the Amen announcement by Bentley, Tine went over to the water bucket to fill the glasses for her and Sylvia and Jonah and Bentley. She stared out the back kitchen window and up the hill over the rail fence and scanned the sky. Nothing did she see except for a clean sky as pure as could be the color of a robin's eggs.

CHAPTER 16

The fall went quickly with all the gathering in to do. Apples and cabbage were buried deep in the barn hallway holes for winter food. Molasses were stored in the cellar. Sweet potatoes and Irish potatoes were in the cellar bins layered in straw. The pigs were slaughtered and hung in side meat and shoulders and ham to cure. After Thanksgiving and Christmas, winter dragged by in endless fireplace fires and big snows.

Spring thaw finally came. With spring blossoms, came time to put out the garden, cows delivered calves, summer work bounced on them. Days went by and Tine stumbled around in the summer work. Her headaches and dizzy spells came often now. They left her dizzy and sick to her stomach, real queasy for hours sometimes. The other day at the well, she had had to sit still on the rock for the longest time to get her energy and bearings back after a bad attack. She even had to break a limb and make a walking stick out of it to steady herself enough to get back to the house with a bucket of water. Thankfully, no one besides Susie and Johnny had taken notice of her spells. Tine was thankful she did not have to answer any questions about them. In fact, she did not have answers to what was going on inside her head and body. Often she wondered if having Johnny was what had caused this sick spells. All she knew was she had started having them right before he was born. Tine knew there would come a day when Bentley would have to know about her head; but, she did not want to worry him about it until she had to tell him.

She had thought of telling Oscar after Callie died; but, Oscar, back then did not need any more burdens than he had. Right now, she was going to keep her sickness with just her and Johnny and Susie. Johnny and Susie just shrugged off the spells and did not seem to worry about them.

Tine was on the foot bridge over the branch with two buckets of water. She had hurried back from her trip to the spring because the clouds overhead looking threatening. The silver maple leaves were tangled upside down in anger at the bursts of quick harsh wind. The silver on the under side of the leaves looked like miniature stars on a dark night against the deep purple storm clouds that were banking up hurriedly in the west.

Tine set her buckets down and turned to the milk gap to let the cows on in the barn early. The air just did not feel right somehow. The air had settled down to a sultry quiet nothingness. Tine let the poles down at the milk gap and all three cows rushed through and twisted their tails high in a rush to the barn hallway. They each halted in front of their usual stalls. The calves gave out low moos of welcome to their moms. Tine put the two fresh cows in with their calves and put the best milking cow in by herself. Tine went to the end of the hallway and studied the sky again. She decided to leave the water buckets and go back and get them later. She hesitated about whether to milk Old Jers now or wait until after supper. She was afraid that Bentley would not be happy with her letting the cows in early like she had.

The dark curly clouds begin racing across the sky under the deep purple clouds. Tine did not like the looks of the sky. The chickens began to gather up under the corn crib in anticipation of an approaching rain storm. Tine grabbed a bucket and began to milk as quickly as she could squeeze milk out of the tits. She would strip her out later. She needed to go onto the house. She felt faint and leaned against the wall as she let the cow back into the stall from the hallway where she had milked her.

Tine worried that Bentley would be upset with her over the early milking.

She could not help from remembering once when he came home and she had forgotten to latch the stalls tight.

When she left the children and went back to latch the stalls she had met Bentley in the hallway of the barn. He was mad at her. He had a wild look in his eyes and he began by shouting out at her, "Tine you don't have enough sense to go straight up. Tine, I swear to God, I can't trust you to do a thing about the farm right can I? I go out logging all day and come home to such doings as this."

Tine had been so shocked at Bentley's tongue lashing that she stumbled dizzily like some old drunk in the barn hallway. She remembered that she had gone to the barn to make sure the animals all had locked stall doors and she knew that she had to double check the crib door to make sure it was buttoned. It was possible for the mules to get into the corn and founder in the night if the doors to the crib were not closed tightly. The mules could take their noses and rub the latches on the doors open. The winter wind had been blowing in a biting blast and lifted her coat tail. Tine remembered how cold she had been that night.

She recalled that she could not believe how Bentley went all to pieces over her forgetting to close that crib door.

After Bentley finished his hollering at her, he flashed that leather whip he had in his hand that he used whenever he slapped the flank of the saddle mule, Ross. Bentley's eyes were fiery. He slung his whip high in the air over her head and made it click like he did when he was training a fiery two year old stead to ride while he had finished his rebuke.

"What in the world did you mean leaving that latch loose like that on the crib? If I had come and caught my best work mule, Ramble, with his head mired up in corn in the crib eating until his heart's content, he would been dead by daybreak. You don't got any idea how a man feels when he comes in late dead likely to find of his best mule with a chance of overeating dying all because of your stupidity," Bentley pronounced with ice hard as ice icicles at ten below zero in the tone of his voice. "You better be glad Ramble did not find that crib door open."

She had gulped and muttered with her head hanging down, "I thought I fixed it tight like you showed me; but, I was coming back to check about it. Bentley raised the whip again and flung it in the air above her head. It cracked like the shot of a .22 rifle. She had seen him crack that whip like that before at the boys.

In fact, he had hit Loy with it once before he caught himself the time Loy threw a rock into his bees and disturbed them. The bees had come out of their hives all stirred up like a stump full of irritated grand-daddies all balled up in a wad. Tine had just stood and stared at Bentley while he was beating Loy with the handle end of the whip. A woman was not supposed to interfere with a man a making his children mind.

"Spare the rod and spoil the child" was what Grandma Stamper had always told her and her momma had said that, too. A man is supposed to rule his roost; Grandpa and Daddy had always done that in their houses. Tine still did not like it when a man used a whip or a cornstalk or something like that to strike out in anger at children. It just didn't make sense to her. A child was not a person all growed up and a child couldn't think like a growed up person and sometimes children just laid down a gap not meaning to do so just like she did not mean to leave that crib door latch loose enough that old Ross or old Ramble could get it open.

Tine had sucked in her stomach and started to try to explain herself to Bentley but decided not to. He never had struck her; but, he had raised his hand like he was going to a time or two like he had that night with that horse whip.

She remembered how scared she had been that he would hit her with that whip.

110

Tine went to bed before Bentley came in from the barn that night. That oldest rooster had been kicked so many times that he stayed clear out of his way all the time now it seemed.

The next morning at the breakfast table Bentley never looked at her or said a word. Tine just went through the motions of cooking his breakfast and packing his lard can dinner bucket with ham and biscuit sandwiches and a piece of dried apple cake for his noon meal. And she filled a quart jar with coffee. Bentley always took him a fruit jar of coffee to drink cold with his meal. Tine couldn't stand cold coffee herself; but, she always fixed it for Bentley. She knew so well what he'd eat she didn't have to ask him a thing about what he wanted to take to the logging woods to eat. That morning she put in an extra country ham sandwich with cornbread a big slice of onion, one of his favorite things to eat in the whole world was a piece of cold cornbread sliced open a big piece of fried ham stuck in the middle of it with a big tater onion slice. Maybe that extra treat would have him in a good humor by the time he got back to the house for supper was what she had hoped for. That morning before he left and again that night when he got home, Bentley had come over to Tine and bent over and glazed the top of her head in a forced kiss. She had not responded; just stood still. She knew he would not mention that he had raised his hand to her. She was always afraid that he would not check himself and go on and lam down and hit her as hard as he did the animals and children. Once he hit Loy with a big piece of oak stove wood.

Loy took it away from his daddy and held up that stick of stove wood high in the air with his eyes glaring at Bentley and said in a low voice as vile sounding as a snake a hissing and said, "Don't you ever raise your hand to me again. I have had the last beating from you that I will ever have. You got that? I ain't going to hit you back this time; but, you had better make damn shore you remember who you are a striking out at the next time if I am the one you air a going to strike. I don't mean to hurt my daddy, but, I will if I have to."

111

Tine didn't say and word, just turned and opened the screen door and picked the baby, Johnny, up out of the floor, sat down in the rocking chair and began to nurse the baby who gobbled and tugged at the nipple, then settled down into a rhythmic feed.

Silent tears slipped down her face and settled in pools on the tops of her breast. The tears on the side of her face just ran right on down and filled the baby's ear. She took hold of the hem of her dress and lifted it to soak up the tears that had fallen onto the nursing infant. The next morning after breakfast, Loy waited until Bentley had the house to go feed and get the mules ready for the logging. Loy had said, "I will not be home anymore, Mom. I am leaving here today. I am eighteen now. There is not enough room in this house for me with Pap throwing fits from time to time. I am going to catch me a ride to town by thumbing down a ride with whoever will stop as soon as I can after I get out to the big road. I am going to go up North and find me a job of some kind. If I cannot find a job, I will come back and sign up for the army. I just ain't ever setting a foot back in that field and have him coming after me like I'm some animal that Dad had trained to work. Let's just put it this way, Momma, I am a kicking out of the hanes today. I won't be a working mule anymore. It ain't the work I mind as you already know. I swear, Momma, I don't want to hurt you or make you cry; but, I have to go now. I am a man full-growed."

Tine recalled every detail of that day.

"Lord, how mercy on us," Tine had smothered out a prayer under her breath. Then she had grabbed Loy and held onto him with both her arms around his and had clinched him to her tightly. She knew Loy had his jaw set and nothing she could say would stop him. And, maybe she had not wanted to stop him. Deep inside her, she had been proud of Loy for standing up for himself. She still was.

"Write me a letter ever week." Tine had demanded of Loy.

Then, she had lifted up her dress tail and unbuttoned the secret money pocket she had sewed in her petticoat and fished out a twenty

112

dollar bill. She had pressed the bill deep into his hand; then, turned abruptly away from him. She remembered that she had to bite her trembling lower lip to keep from breaking down right there in front of Loy. She had sat down by the churn and lifted the dash and started to churn in a sustained rhythm. She had not looked up as the screen door slammed behind Loy; but, her chest had heaved up and down as she breathed in difficult breathes, in jerks, like pulling morning glories off corn stalks in October.

For some reason, her chest felt that tight right now.

She remembered praying hard all that day.

"Dear God take care of him for me," she had whispered over and over. The afternoon sun had filtered through the window and caressed her brow and hands as she prayed.

Tine hugged herself up real tight and clutched her coat together to keep the cold wind out. She hurried to double check all the doors of the stalls and the crib to see that they were latched real tight. And, she vowed to herself, "I dare, just dare Bentley to ever raise a whip towards me ever again like he did that night."

Tine had gotten used to Loy's being gone from home. He brought a woman back from up North. The army did not take him. It had worried Tine that Loy had been hanging out with an old boot legger, Max Simpsom. His wife, Elvina, had told Tine about Loy's taking to drinking bunches since they moved back home to the country.

Tine worried about Loy and his children. It worried her that the army did not take him due to his high blood pressure. Loy was too young to be turned down by the army. If Bentley worried about Loy and his family, he never mentioned it. Tine wondered if Bentley did not go by and see them on his produce runs. Loy did not come around much to see them.

Tine's dizzy spells had started increasing until it seemed like she had one every day now. Sometimes her head hurt so badly that she would have to go lie down awhile to make them go away. Susie knew she was having a hard time with them headaches; but, Johnny was always out under the trees drawing or carving or writing stories when he could fine a piece of paper of any kind or a knife sharp enough to cut wood. He could make something out of nothing. Most of it was trifling stuff; but, his head was full of his own thoughts; if he was not doing his work, Bentley laid out for him, he was occupying himself. He was just an older child who seemed to have a grown up mind and words. Johnny did not take notice of her spells. Susie would pull the curtains together and make it sort of darker so the outside light would not make her head and eyes hurt any worse. Susie would iron or do needle works while Tine laid down to give the pains time to move on out of her head.

"God Bless that sweet child of mine," Tine thought.

Susie had not breathed to a soul, not even to Lester, that Tine had had to take to her bed sometimes in the daytime.

Since Susie had mailed that engagement ring back to Wade Elroy year in a "Dear John" letter, Lester, was coming to see her two or three times a week now ever since they had met at the kissing party. Bentley said that he was beginning to smell a wedding brewing. Susie had not said a thing to Tine about marrying, yet. Right now until these sick spells quit coming, Tine was glad that Susie was sticking around.

Johnny, with his back all twisted and crippled, would never be able to help as good as the other children and Susie could. He had seemed like a big robust baby, but, the older he grew, his back was turning toward the ground all bent over like. He complained all the time about his back being stiff and not being able to lift stuff. Bentley thought he was just trying to get out of his work; but, Tine had watched him close when no one else was looking at him. The child would have to set a bucket of water down three or four times and rest between the well and the house. The house and the well were no more than five hundred feet apart. He could not hold out to do a thing for some reason. But, he could draw for hours and hours. Bentley said that Johnny's dawning wouldn't ever amount to a thing. He said that Johnny ought to get out in the fields

and the garden and help Susie more while Bentley was gone on his produce wagon trying to make us extra money. Tine knew Johnny couldn't
handle heavy man's work; so, she let Johnny go to the house and rest
when he said he needed to. It was hard to determine how much work a
child could do when he complained all the time. Johnny limped, too.

Tine did not think he was faking a thing about his back hurting all
the time. Nobody around had ever seen such thing as this affliction as
Johnny's.

Whenever she could catch Dr. Jed around in the neighborhood,
she would ask him about her head aches and Johnny's troubles with is
back not growing up straight. Her head problems and Johnny's being
so puny, all of it just didn't seem right somehow.

Tine knew that there way not way to get to a big city and find a good
doctor for either one of them. Bentley would never agree to spending
money and going far away for doctoring. He thought that Dr. Jed was
the only doctor a body ever needed. Bentley didn't know there was a
thing wrong with her and he didn't think there was a thing wrong with
Johnny either.

When she had asked him to take Johnny to the doctor Bentley had
yelled out, "I don't have a bit of faith in them doctors. All they do is
take your money and you are right where you started. If the Lord don't
heal you, there's not much nobody else can do for you either. Things
will change. They always get better if you leave them alone. Johnny
just needs to stay right out there and keep working. Hard work will
help instead of hurt anybody unless they are dying. You can't help a
body anyway if he is a dying."

Tine thought that Bentley was wrong. Doctors and other people
who had schooling had read up on things and knew things they didn't.

When Tine got out of Bentley's hearing she said to herself. "I will
speak with Dr. Jed whenever he was in the neighborhood again."

Tine knew that Dr. Jed would have an idea what was wrong with
her. She wanted to talk to him about Johnny's growing a bent back like

115

he was. Even the Bible taught that if you would seek you would find. Tine thought that meant that a body ought to hunt out the truth of everything and understand help it as much as they could; not, just leave complicated problems alone. Seems to her in her head, it meant more than just a looking to God for salvation like all the preachers and Sunday school teachers always said it meant.

CHAPTER 17

Besides worrying about what in the world was wrong with her head and Johnny's back, it grieved Tine that Sylvie and Jonah had taken the advice of their citified kinfolks who had moved away to find work. All the folks that had moved away to the city painted up of life in the big city being a whole heap better than life in the country. Tine did not see that moving up there had done a thing but hurt them and their children. Tine thought that it seemed like years since they had all left home. All the women who had move up North were always bragging about not having to stand over an old hot wood stove to cook and stuff like that. Tine did not mind her stove. In the summer, she always got the cooking done early and got out of the hot kitchen in the afternoons and evenings. Tine knew she did not ever want to leave the place.

Jonah and Sylvie believed that they could do more for her two children, Cecil and Cecilia, since they had moved away to town. The school they went to was right on the same block as where they lived. They did not have to walk a long ways to school like they did here in the country. The school was just across the street from their apartment, three rooms in an old hospital building that had been remodeled. Jonah rode the city bus across town and back every day to and from work. He had saved up enough money to buy an old Buick car after he had found Sylvia and the children a place to live. That's when Jonah had come and moved them away. Tine hid in the back room and sobbed her heart out the day they left the valley. She still could not understand why Jonah wanted to go away and find work like he did. There was plenty of work on the farm, it seemed to Tine.

Cecilia was in the sixth grade and she wrote to her Grandma Tine every week. Her teacher had told her to write real letters to someone; so, Cecilia had chosen to write to her Grandma Tine. The mule mail delivery came every day no matter how cold or how muddy the road happened to be. Tine watched for Hubert, the mail carrier, especially on Fridays when the letters from Cecilia usually arrived. Cecilia was the one who spoke the real truth about life in the far away city to Tine.

This Friday, Hubert, handed her the letter and said his usually greeting, "It's a good morning, ain't it, Clementine."

Very few people ever called Tine, Clementine, her given name that her sister Carlista could not pronounce as a little girl. Carlista could only say "Tine." So, the whole family deemed her Tine from that time on. Oscar in their private meetings called her Clementine. Tine shook off the emotion at the memory of Oscar's endearments.

"Looks like that grand child of yours has sent you another letter of news from Sylvia and Jonah and them up North there in the big city." That was what Hubert always said when he reached down out of the saddle pockets and pulled out the hand printed envelope addressed:

Grandma Clementine Ferguson

Skip Rock, Kentucky

Tine always smiled at Cecilia's scribble- grade-school handwriting. Tine always got a kick out of the way the address lines ran sideways down the envelope. She knew Cecilia had addressed it all by herself since it was crooked like. Cecilia was old enough to go to the post office and get stamps. She earned a little money from baby sitting three children next door while they were waiting on their mom to come in from work. The children that Cecilia babysat had a daddy that had to leave to go on the night shift before their mom got in from cooking at the school cafeteria. Cecilia had written that they had asked her to stand watch over their children for about three hours every day.

Tine was proud that her granddaughter could be trusted to take care of strangers' children like that.

Tine opened the letter, but, not with her regular glee at getting a letter from the children. Cecilia had been writing some strange stuff about Sylvie lately. Tine had not told Bentley or Sally or anyone about it. Cecilia had said that her Mommy has been listening to her friend, this woman named Daisy Kaye, who lived down the hall, talk about witches and demons and stuff and that Mommy had a started to believe her and to believe that both Daisy Kaye and her Mom, too, had some sort of special powers. Cecilia had written that her mom was never home when she and Cecil came home from school and that Jonah daddy was always working overtime. Jonah never got home until seven o'clock pm. Cecilia and Cecil had been cooking supper every night after Cecilia got through her babysitting job at five pm. They did not tell their daddy about their Mommy and Daisy Kaye because they knew he would be upset and yell at Sylvie and threaten to quit his city job and move back down to the country where they did not have good heat or an indoor toilet like they did in the city.

Tine remembered that time when Sylvie and Jonah were at the house and Sylvie had talked about seeing that angel a going up the rail fence. A puzzled frown wrinkled her brow. Now, all this talk about witches seemed worse than talk about angels. Tine did not know one thing about witches. She did not know much about angels either except for what the Bible said. The biggest thing she could remember about angels was that the preacher was always preaching about the one that appeared at Christ's tomb for the preacher's Easter sermon. And Tine always read in the Bible at Christmas to the children about the angels that came in the sky and announced Christ's being born.

"Seemed like angels only had to do with Jesus Christ's stuff and not with people's business." Tine muttered.

Haints and witches were always just for jokes at Halloween. Nobody around here had ever taken them as real so what in the world was Sylvie doing listening to stuff like that. Tine wished that Jonah knew about all this foolish sounding stuff that Sylvie had got mixed up in. Tine didn't dare write back to Cecilia a thing about her reports in the letter. She would have to tell Sally about it when she seen her. Sally would help her figure out what to do. Sylvie was always having a make believe friend or telling big wild tales, all made up herself when she was little. Maybe this was sort of like that. Maybe she and that woman, Daisy Kaye, were just making up stories because they were bored. Tine knew they did not have work to do much like country women did. All the old people always said, "A idle mind is the devil's workshop." It sounded to Tine from Cecilia's letters that Sylvie had gotten into an awful lot of the devil's work with her idle mind. Sylvie needed a garden and some cows and chickens to take care of that would help keep her mind occupied. Maybe it would be better if they a moved back down close to the family. Sylvie did not say one foolish word until Jonah took her off to live in Cincinnati in that old building with people living right on top of each other and no yard or shade trees in the summer or nothing. That type of living would drive the best crazy.

Tine broke open the letter and read:

"Grandma Tine
    Mommy is getting worser with all that witch talk.
    She keeps dolls that she sticks pins into for some reason.
    She won't talk about it. She keeps the dolls all to herself.
    She won't let me or Cecil touch them. She takes them back
to Daisy Kaye afore daddy gets home everyday. My teacher said
I ought to tell you and Grandpa.

Me and Cecil don't know what to do. Actlly, Cecil don't let it bother him

He just goes off down to the street to play except he is always a fighting. Cecil, he, even hit a girl day before yesterday. She told his teacher that Cecil was the one who blacked her eye up good. When the teacher found out the inncedent tooked place on the street at our building and not at school, all Cecil's teacher said was_____I don't want to hear about your fights at home there is enough of them at school___I ' amm trying very hardto keep Cecil out of trouble but he don't pay much attention to me All he says is You ain't my boss.

Mommy don't get after him no time That makes me so mad

And, I won't tell daddy cause he would beat him to death with his belt or something like that.I like my school.I like my teacher.

I shore do wish I lived clost to you and grandpa school will be out soon and we

Want to come you again when daddy gets his vacation

I love you your granddaughter

Signed,

Cecilia.

Tine folded the letter and put it inside her petticoat pocket and buttoned it down tight. She would show it to Sally and then write back to Cecilia. There was no way she could get up there to talk to Sylvie and look into this mess with Sylvie and try to figure out what in this world was in Sylvie's head.

Had her girl lost her mind and her a grown woman? Tine had no answers. If this news about Sylvie believing in witches and angels got out, people would say that Sylvie was "teched in the head" and that would bring disgrace to the family to have her called a crazy person.

With weary steps Tine pushed herself up the slope of the yard and into the house.

Tine went into the side room and got down by the trunk. That old black travel trunk Bentley had before they married lent itself to her as a prayer bench.

Bentley held that they might use the trunk if they ever needed to go away from the homeplace and look for work. Tine knew Bentley would never leave. Too often he would say as if to himself, "The relatives of mine, including my Sylvie and her Jonah, can have it and their fotched on ways. That city life does not got a bit of appeal for me."

Tine had never been to the city; so, she just agreed with Bentley. Tine knew that there was no place on earth as beautiful and calm as the ravine around the black gum well, and there could never be any more pure or cold water than the well provided. She did not want to live anywhere else; this was home.

Tine got down on her knees. She didn't have to read that letter again in order to know what to pray about. She could remember every word of it. She could ask the Lord to help the children and Sylvie and Jonah.

Tine poured her heart out in almost groans as she prayed, "Father, God, take care of Sylvie and Cecil and Cecilia, and Jonah. Get them old ideas about witches out of Sylvie's head, Lord. You have all power; so, you take care of her Lord. Lord, you gave her to me and I did the best I could by her. Lord, you lead Jonah to see the light and do what is right for his family. Lord, lay it on his heart to bring them home. Lord, heal Sylvie. Oh, Lord, heal Sylvie and, Lord, let me ask you again to take good care of my grandbabies that I can't see but once a year. You know I love them all Lord, and I know Lord, that you love them even more than I do, ten thousand times more. Thank you, Lord. Thank you."

Tine started to get up from her knees but, her head spun around and around.

She could not see a thing in the room. She felt the trunk and turned around and sat down on it. She held on to each end of the trunk to steady herself until she got her bearings. She could not, to save her life, figure out where these blind eyed-dizzy spells were coming from all of them so close together lately. The children and Bentley had not caught on yet how bad the head ache and dizzy spells had gotten, even though, sometimes she got hit with a horrible one right in front of them all. She had not had one that had lasted long enough for them to notice. Thank goodness she had not staggered plum down with one of them. That day coming in from the garden with the big bucket of beans she and Susie had picked, she had a really, really bad one and stumbled coming up through the yard next to that old silver maple tree. She had caught herself against that tree instead of a falling down to the ground. When Susie asked her what the matter was, Tine had lied to her. Tine told Susie that she reckoned that she had caught her shoe heel on them old roots sticking up and running atop of the ground. She had told Susie that they ought to get Johnny and Bentley to haul in some dirt and even up the ground around that old tree before some of them stumbled on them old roots and got hurt badly. Tine kept going on about how the roots were dangerous, especially at night, and when one was not paying a whole lot of attention to where he was a going like, she had been as she stumbled against the tree.

Susie took her lie as the truth and said, "I think you are right about them old roots sticking up that way, Momma."

Tine glanced at the clock. She needed to start a fire in the stove and start supper. It wouldn't be long until Susie and Johnny and Bentley would be coming to the house. They'd be hungry after they had chopped corn all day long like this. She was bound not to bring up that letter from Cecilia even though she wished she could. There was not a bit a use of causing them to worry.

CHAPTER 18

Fall came and went.

It was Christmas Eve. Tine had her oven hot enough to bake. Methodically, she worked in the kitchen and hummed "O Beautiful Star of Bethlehem, shinning afar through shadows dim" while she took inventory of whether she had all the jams and jellies in from the cellar that she wanted for the Christmas morning breakfast. Tine realized that she was holding out without a single one of them pain flashes that sometimes brought her to her knees in spite of all she could do to stay standing up straight. Bentley had gone and taken the children up the hill and around the ridge to the one-room school for the Christmas play. Johnny had drawn pictures of the first Christmas story for the teacher to put up on the wall behind the students as they acted out the Bible Christmas story. Tine had begged off going along with them by saying that she needed to do some baking to get ready for the Christmas dinner day after tomorrow. The real reason she had not gone was she was deeply afraid that she might get one of the headaches and dizzy spells. Tine had a dreadful fear that she might fall out of her chair right there in the middle of the floor and draw attention to herself and mess up the whole Christmas program.

Lester had picked up Susie to go to the Christmas program with him. Susie had climbed on right behind him on the mule. That was a dead-for-certain sign that they would be marrying soon. No woman who wasn't "promised" would ride on a mule holding on to a man's waist if she had not said yes to the question. Tine wondered about when or if Ira might be getting married. He had been going down to the Childers place for five years now. She wondered if Mirara would say yes if Ira asked her to marry him. Ira was five years younger than Mirara. He was the best looking man in these parts. If she were getting away up into her twenties and still single like Mirara, she would not refuse Ira if he asked her to marry him. Of course, Tine realized that she was Ira's mother and didn't think real straight about her boy's being a good choice for a husband.

Anyway, Tine thought, "I like Mirara the most of all the possible in-laws so far."

She forgot about Lester and when she thought of him, she thought that Lester just seems like one of mine already even if he's not an in-law yet. Tine said to herself, "I'll bet a nickel Lester and Susie will wed before next year's Christmas. They are just too thick as Bentley would say."

Tine turned off the radio when the news came on. She hated to listen to stories that this war would take all the boys around away overseas. But, Susie's man, Lester, and Jonah were all too old to have to go fight. At least her girls would be spared having to send a husband off to World War II with children home to take care of all by themselves.

It was Christmas and Tine was not going to think on all that war stuff right now. Tine headed to the kitchen and punched up the stove again and went to work laying out the stuff that she needed to make dried apple hand pies. She could make her special spiced white sugar gravy to have to heat up and pour over the pies hot on Christmas at the noon meal. Her mouth watered just thinking about how good the pies would be when she dipped up her special sauce and poured over them for dessert. All the children had always loved her dried apple pies and she wouldn't let Christmas go without them no matter how tired and sick she felt. Tine commenced to put her apples on to cook and measured out the ingredients to make the dough she would wrap the cooked apples in before she put them into the oven. She heard someone on the front porch and crossed the living room from the kitchen and opened the door to find Ira and Mirara at the door.

"Me and Mirara is getting married tonight, right here in the house. Mom, get your flour-covered apron off. Preacher Johnson is at school for the Christmas play and he is a coming home with Pap and Johnny in the wagon. Lester and Susie will be right behind them. There is going to be a wedding here tonight!" Ira reported in a joyful voice.

Tine grabbed Mirara and hugged her tight." Well, I'll be. If that doesn't just about tickle me to death." Tine announced to them. Then, Tine turned and hugged her sweet, precious beautiful Ira real tight.

"Let's hurry and get them pies in the oven. Mirara, just go ahead and hang up your wraps. Are you a staying here tonight or are you going back to your daddy's?" Tine rushed the words out.

"I reckon' we are going to stay here tonight if it's all right with you all. Ira told Dad and Mom to come on over about noon tomorrow and stay for a wedding supper even if it Christmas Eve. Ira said your Christmas dinner can just double as our wedding dinner. Ira's plans are fine with me if it's okay by you. My brothers and sisters and their families don't ever come to Dad and Mom's until Christmas Day for supper anyway, so it will work out good if it's okay with you all," Mirara timidly conversed with Tine.

"Why it is fine for your folks to come tomorrow, honey. Sally will be here early in the morning. That man of hers does not ever come with her. He won't leave their place even at Christmas. But, he don't fuss a bit that Sally comes to see us. She comes every Christmas Eve morning and leaves Christmas Day in time to get home before dark. She never misses no matter how cold or how much snow might fall. She just puts on her rubber boots and heavy clothes and comes right on. One year it was so cold, she had two pairs of man's underwear under her clothes and stockings. I swear she is a sight. Nobody could ask to have a better girl than Sally. Susie has already invited Lester to spend Christmas Day with us. The rest of them don't come until the Sunday after Christmas. There is not time enough to get them the news now anyway." Tine was breathless with the excitement of the wedding.

Ira rushed to open the door when footsteps sounded from crossing the front porch. Susie, Lester and Johnny and Bentley came inside.

"We did not stick around for socializing. We had a wedding to go to," Johnny burst out and Mom, they loved my drawings," He added.

"Put some more wood on the fires in each room, Ira. I will turn up the flames on the coal oil lamps. There are some candles we can light, too, when it gets time to say the ceremony. Who is a going to stand up with you two, Lester and Susie?" Tine blustered out the instructions and the question.

Ira said, "I like Lester so much, I wouldn't think of having anyone else and Mirara likes Susie so much." The preacher is what we had been a waiting on. I believe I hear him over at the barn now. Let's go help him put his mule up."

Mirara followed Tine to the back side room. Tine took a long purple and yellow flowered calico long-sleeved dress that she saved for special occasions. She let her every day dress fall to her feet and lifted her church dress over her head.

"Ooops, Mirara, will you help me get it down over my big head of hair so I won't have to take my hair down? After I get it all buttoned up, you can tie my sash in the back for me," Tine excitedly addressed her soon to be daughter-in-law.

Mirara gently tugged the dress down over Tine's head and hair trying to not mess up a single strand of hair. Tine felt a pang and went a little dizzy. She reached over and held on to the head railing of the wrought iron bedstead and steadied herself until the flash subsided and her eyes cleared. Tine hoped Mirara had not noticed her wobbling.

"Am I ready?" she asked.

"Yes, you are, and you look mighty pretty, Tine. I am so proud to join your family. I have loved your Ira for a long time now," Mirara hugged Tine as she talked.

"Well, I am glad to hear that come from ye, Mirara. If Ira is ever not good to you, if he ever raises a hand toward you, you just run off right then and come to me, and I'll hide you from him, you hear?" Tine instructed.

Mirara looked startled at Tine's comments. She answered, "I don't think you will ever have to worry about that, Tine, Ira ain't ever been anything but good to me."

She took hold of Tine's hand and together they went to the living room where Ira and the preacher and Lester and Susie were standing in front of the fire. Tine sat down in the rocking chair next to Bentley.

The preacher said, "Now, that we are all here and ready, let's start with a word of prayer."

Tine bowed her head but did not close her eyes. She saw Ira reach and take a hold of Mirara's hand.

Tine prayed her own prayer and did not hear a word the preacher said. She prayed, "Lord, I am afraid for my boys. Oh, God, please spare my children from ever having to leave this creek and go to fight across the waters."

As Preacher Johnson droned out the traditional words…"God made a woman to be a man's help mate"…Tine looked at Bentley. Tine could not believe that they married so long ago. Oscar had helped her to walk with Bentley during that awful time when the baby and Eunice died and Johnny was little.

She had to push Oscar out of her mind or she would burst out crying right there in front of them all in the middle of the wedding. She swallowed her tears right back down.

Oscar would never be back home. She might as well stop suffering over his not being around.

"A body come into the world alone and a body goes out alone," was what Grandma Ferguson told her after Papaw Ferguson died and left her

129

young with her children barely grown enough to take care of themselves. The older Tine got, the more that talk her Grandma told her about living life on one's own two feet made more and more sense to her.

"Reckon the only thing Bentley ever thought of was work and money. He forgot that a marriage needed to be tended just like a good garden to grow and flourish. The garden of their marriage just about dried up except for taking care of and feeding the children. When Johnny left home, if he was ever able to go out on his own, she wondered what Bentley would be like then. Bentley had not been the same, just sad all the time and not a saying much no time since Leonard went into the army and Oscar had left for Ohio. Ira would be the next one to go off and leave them. The army would call on him sooner or later; but, she not going to think about that now. It was Christmas Eve and Ira was finally getting married. Mirara would make him a fine woman."

CHAPTER 19

Two weeks after Ira and Mirara married, Ira came in the kitchen door and let the screen door slam hard behind him. He didn't say a word; but fear and astonishment were mixed in his face. Tine did not dare ask what was wrong. She got up from the chair beside the churn and moved to the stove and lifted the coffee pot and went to the cabinet and took out two coffee cups. Her hands shook.

"Here Ira, sit down to the table. I will pour us a cup of coffee. It is real chilly out there today."

Ira pulled out the chair that he most usually used at the table before he left home. He sipped on the cup of steaming hot coffee in nervous jerks.

"This is good stuff, Mom," he volunteered about the coffee. "I had to come here first, Mom. I could not bear to go tell her myself." As he spoke the last word, he laid an envelope on the table with trembling fingers.

Tine knew what it was. "Your draft notice?" she questioned. Without waiting for an answer, she pinned him down with the next question. "When do you have to report for duty?" She asked struggling to keep trembling out of her voice.

"I have just two weeks, Mom, just two weeks. I just have two weeks with my wife before I have to leave her," Ira's voice broke as he talked.

Tine had known that Ira would be taken. Maybe, just maybe, Ira would be lucky as Leonard had and get to stay on a base in the states and not have to go fight. She was wringing her hands with anxiety under the table so Ira would not see how nervous and scared she was.

"If two weeks is all you got, then, get on down to Mirara's Pappy's house and go to Mirara and get the bad news over. All I know is that we will pray and pray for you everyday," she offered in a comforting tone.

You can tell Mirara that I know that Bentley will want her to come stay with us while you are gone if she wants to do that. I would like to have her here with us."

Ira took strength from his mother's words and instructions. He slurped the rest of his coffee down before he hurried away to go to tell Mirara.

"Mom, I want to come back over here tomorrow night. We will split time between her folks and my folks until I go; then, she can decide what she wants to do." Ira's voice cracked on the last word.

As soon as Bentley left the yard, Tine grabbed her egg basket and headed to the chicken house. It was the closest building to her house. She ran to the chicken house as if she might be a going to put out a fire. Once inside the chicken house, she closed the door behind her. She set the egg basket down. Her knees wobbled. She sank down in desperate fear. Then she fell forward on her face in the dried chicken manure. Dust and feathers flew up in the air as chickens squawked in alarm at her intrusion. One big rooster flapped his wings and flew up on the roost turning over the watering trough as he pushed off to fly up. Tine lay with her face in the dusty dung. She stretched her arms out in front of her face in fear and pain that she would loose her boy to death in this old war being fought across the waters. She had seen too many mothers find their son or son's name posted on the court house wall on Saturday afternoon down at the county seat. In her head, she could hear women's screams when the names of their sons fell on the list as dead or missing in action. She squeezed the dried manure in her hands as if a handful of chicken excrement would aid and assist her in letting go of Ira. She began to vomit. She could not cry. She could only gag out her agony. She lay there and gagged and vomited until she felt faint and lifeless. The chickens grew used to her and went about their business of pecking at corn grains from the morning's feeding. After what seemed like a long, long time, Tine reached up to a roosting poll and pulled herself up onto her feet. She beat the dust and feathers off her apron and dress. She took her apron tail and swiped at the dirt on her face. She picked up the egg basket and went in slow lifeless motion around to each nest and robbed it of its eggs that the hens had deposited that day. When the eggs were gathered, she opened the chicken house door and went out into the blinding cold winter daylight that was as clear as a pane of polished glass.

She vowed that she would not get ahead of God. That she would think the best until the war ended and Ira was back home.

When Bentley came to the house that night, Tine announced the news that Ira would be leaving in two weeks. Bentley just picked up his hat and started back to the barn. He did stop on his way as Tine reached out to hug him. He was speechless. His face was toward the floor.

For the first time in years, Tine spoke up in a firm voice, "Bentley, stop and let's hold each other. He did and clumsily put his arms around her shoulders. She felt his body shake against hers as they clung to each other. Neither one of them cried.

That night Tine rolled and tumbled all night long. She could hear Bentley doing the same thing across the room in the other bed.

The next morning the mail man had a letter addressed to Tine. It was Jonah and Sylvie's return address but Tine knew it was not written by Cecilia or Sylvie. She tore open the envelope as she walked towards the house.

The letter read:

Dear Clementine,

I wanted to share some news with you. I am hoping you get this by Christmas. I made Old Man Jesse Pennington an offer on his place when we went over there, me and Bentley, to see him last summer when we was down there a visitin. Well, he has wrote to me and accepted my offer. I am sending him a check to hold the place for me until the weather breaks and I can get down there to make the deed. I will have the rest of the money to pay him about April. He don't want to move in with his girl until summer anyway; but, he wrote that this is the last winter that he can stay all by hisself. He is too far up in years to farm any more too. We will be a movin back to be your neighbor again as soon as the children are finished with his year's schooolin. I have hated having to have Sylvie and the children live up here but I have been able to save enough money to buy us that place. No one of us likes it here; so, we are comeing home.

Bentley knowed that I might be going to get the place; but, he promised me that he would let me tell you myself. So, you can tell him now that the deal is for shore on. I know you all have worried about us up here; but, we are a comin' home for good.

Your son-in-law, Jonah

CHAPTER 20

Bentley seemed more weary than usual as he came in from the produce run. He got a long drink in the gourd dipper from the bucket of water on the sink. Then, he pulled a chair from under the table and filled his plate from the bowls on the table. He was about half way through the meal before he spoke a word.

Then, he began, "There was a terrible murder last night over on Fall's Branch. Seems like a bunch of drunks got in a spat over that Lindsay woman of ill refute where bad doings is always going on. That dull-witted Arbuckle boy hangs around that woman all the time. He did not like for men to come to see her even though he knew he was not the only one that could have her from the start. Well, there was some harsh words said and the Arbuckle flashed a knife; did not cut anybody or nothing. But everybody knows that Hoss Benjamin has been a going over there to see that woman for years. If his woman knows anything about his being over there so often she never lets on. Well, anyway, Hoss run Arbuckle off and threatened whopping him right there at the woman's house. Right around midnight James Foxworthy was driving two cows down the dry creek bed home. They had got out and he was a taking them home. Well, his horse spooked down about a mile from Lindsay's house. He got off his horse and lit the lantern and could not believe his eyes. Arkbuckle was laying there with his head kicked in. He was stone dead. So, Foxworthy left his cows and let them run wild and went back to his house and got his boy to go with him. They rode as hard and as fast as they could over to Sherriff Masters's house and woke him up and told him that he needed to come quick."

Tine held her breath. She feared that Loy have might been over there. Nobody ever said anything about him ever a being over there; but, if he was, he wouldn't a hurt a soul drunk or sober. But, she did pose the question. "Do you know if Loy was at home or not last night?"

Bentley answered her questions with these words tumbling on top of each other, "I drove by Loy's on my way home and stopped pretending to see if they all was fairing all right, the little ones and all, and to tell the boys to come down and get a gallon of milk now that there is plenty here with the heifer being fresh now and having weaned her calf. Loy volunteered that he was home by nine o'clock last night that Max had dropped him off on his way to Fall's Branch to deliver a big bull calf over that way. Max was going to spend the night with his cousin, James, down on Lower Fall Branch. When I told Loy the High Sheriff and two deputies were combing the whole area and questioning everybody who might have an inkling of an idea why anyone would want to kill Arbuckle, Loy just replied that it sounded like a bad piece of business any way you looked at it. He seemed as stunned and baffled as I am at who would have beat that boy to death and why. Looks to me like that ought to be a lesson to Loy that he needs to stay completely away from them kinds of doings. I know he wouldn't go there unless Max got him drunk and then he might not resist going along with a bunch," Bentley spouted out.

Tine verabilized her relief that Loy was not anywhere around that place last night, by saying, "Praise be to God that Loy was at home last night."

The family ate the rest of their evening meal in silence. Tine thought to herself as she lifted her fork up to her face, "I don't think I could have stood any more bad news."

That night Tine was restless and did not sleep well. She kept on having bad dreams. Oscar was there in the dreams; then, he disappeared. Tine's dream was so confusing she thought she was at the black gum well and in the cemetery at the same time. When Tine woke up she was tired.

CHAPTER 21

It was the first Sunday of June already. The sweet country air was filled with festive movement. Tine and Bentley and the children were moving quickly around the house in anticipation of the day's events. The family had decided last year to have the dinner down at Bentley and Tine's house instead of up on the hill at the graveyard.

Bentley had offered to set up tables in the front yard under the silver maples. That way they could have the food on tables instead of on quilt pallets on the ground at the graveyard the way they had always been doing the dinner. The summer sun had dried up the dirt road enough so that cars could travel right down the hill to the house. The Indiana and Ohio relatives in their sleek new cars were sprinkled in uneven parking slots across the front yard. Some had been pulled right out into the open field that made for a grass parking lot. It was like having a Christmas party in warm weather. Tine, Susie and Sally had been up since daylight killing chickens and dressing them and cooking them and frying the last ham. Sally had taken it on herself to kill two big young rosters to fry them in a huge black skillet; she made chicken gravy to go over the mashed potatoes. Tine and her girls had baked dried apple stack cakes and had made apple pies and potato salad on Friday and Saturday so as they would just have to finish up the noonday meal this am. Now, all they had to do was make dumplings and bake biscuits and cornbread to be done just in time to set on the table, hot, to go with the other dishes. Tine had put fresh ironed sheets for table clothes on the rough lumber saw-horse tables that Bentley and the boys erected on Saturday evening right before dark.

This morning Bentley carried every chair in the house out in the yard. There would not be enough chairs but the children and young people wouldn't mind sitting on the steps of the porch, or standing along the sides of the porches and eat their meals while standing up using the porch floor as a makeshift type of table.

Tine instructed Johnny to get the water for the water bucket table that Bentley had moved off the back porch into the yard in the shade of the big maples.

Tine added in a firm demanding tone, "Johnny, keep an eye on the water buckets all day and make sure you keep them filled with fresh well water. Make certain anyone can have a fresh dipper of water anytime all day."

Wagons pulled with mules begin to arrive real close to noon. Rows of food lined the tables as women carried in pots from their wagons. The tables grew to look like a meal fit for a king.

Bentley took all the mules that pulled the wagons of the local folks to the barn and put them in the stalls to rest and eat while the family visited and ate. Tine sent some of the boy cousins to help Johnny go draw about four or five buckets of fresh water and set them on the table. The main table had mashed potatoes and canned green beans. There were jars of homemade pickles, strawberry preserves and pear preserves and blackberry jams and jellies to be spread on biscuits with homemade butter. There were bowls of cream style corn poured out of last year's half gallon jars and flavored with butter and white sauce and pepper. Big bowls of cooked cabbage from this year's garden were also added to the bounty. Susie brought every plate in the house and every fork and spoon, too, out to the tables. The women all in their pretty starched calico aprons over their Sunday dresses gathered outside in the yard, a hint for the children to stop playing, and a signal for the men out under the trees smoking and talking to stop and be silent.

Tine announced. "We have dinner ready. As soon as Bentley says the blessing, everybody come and help yourselves. We'll let the men go first, then the children. Bentley, go ahead with grace."

Bentley looked around and surveyed the crowd. Then, he announced to the crowd of relatives assembled, "Well, let's turn the job of saying grace over to Lester. Lester has asked Susie to marry him real soon like and he'll be the newest member of this family. Go ahead, Lester, lead us in prayer."

Susie smiled at her father for approving Lester and her plan to be married. She knew he really liked Lester to ask him to pray in front of all the folks like that. She knew some of the families were talking behind their backs about Lester's being older than her and having been married before. Susie thought they should stick to their own business. She was a going to marry Lester no matter what anybody said.

Lester, in a shy embarrassed tone, quickly droned out a type of uniform prayer, "Our Father we thank ye for this food. Bless the hands that prepared it. Bless it to the nourishment of our bodies. Amen."

With the last breath of the prayer, men grabbed hold of a plate and dug into the bowls and mounted up their plates and found themselves a place to sit and to eat.

Immediately, following them, came the children holding their breaths that there would be a fried chicken leg left by the time they got to the platter of fried chicken. Every child grabbed a sugar cookie ahead for fear that the cookies might all get be gone if they waited to come back for dessert later. After the children and men ate, the women gathered up all the empty dirty plates and forks and spoons and headed back into the kitchen to wash the dishes so they'd have clean plates to eat on themselves. They knew many of the bowels would be empty by the time they got to eat, but, they always just ate whatever food was left even if it were cold food by the time they got to sit down to the table.

Tine said to the women, "Just go on out and set down and visit and rest in the shade. The men have wandered off to the barn to talk men talk about the crops and the animals so there's a plenty of chairs for you now. The children are all off in the woods over by the spring talking and a playing now. I'll wash and dry these dishes and bring out a whole stack of clean plates for us in just a few minutes. I saved some hot water on the stove in the dish pan to rinse them in, too."

Osie came into the kitchen and offered, "Aunt Clementine, let me help you with the dishes."

Tine hated the way the folks came back trying to speak differently than they had spoken at home. Osie had always just called her Tine like everyone else until she went off and got herself a city job and city man.

"I reckon" she thinks 'Aunt Clementine' is proper or something," Tine thought to herself.

"Well, get you a clean apron off that nail there by the back door. You don't want to get your fancy store-bought dress messed up now with no dish water splatters." Tine spoke politely.

She would put up with Osie and her new fangled ways for a short time. At least Osie only came home once a year at Decoration and thank goodness she stayed with Mam and Pap when she made her visiting rounds. Tine washed and Osie dried the dishes.

Osie mentioned the crops and the garden looked good, then she told Tine, "I still miss my garden. There just taint no ground to grow nothing in town where we are. I think country food just taste so much better than what we buy in them big stores away from here."

Tine did not respond. "Tain't must be some sort of made up word Osie made up and used trying to be proper and all citified again." Tine thought.

Tine had never been to a store except the close by for stuff she couldn't raise like soda, salt, sugar and a few things like that.

The two of them washed dishes right on in silence.

"I noticed Cousin Vina didn't say much today. Her man is still away a fighting in this awful war. I guess that is heavy on her mind," Tine filled up empty space with talk.

Osie lowered her voice. "I think it's a lot deeper than that. Did you know that she came Christmas before last to visit Arvella after she moved out from Oscar and Marjorie's?"

Tine held a stone face as she listened.

"Well, Vina brought that little toddler of a girl all the way up there arcoss the state on one of them old buses. Arvella said that they stayed a full week. Both Vina and her little girl had to sleep on the living room couch because Arvella just has little bitty old apartment in an old run down building next to the new hospital building where she cleans. Well, Arvella hinted that when Vina got there that she noticed how tired looking that Vina was. She had put on weight, too, since Ance went off to fight in Italy. After a couple of days, she broke down on Arvella and cried and cried. Vina told Arvella that she needed doctor help. Vina added to Arvella that she had heard that you could get help in the city from doctors so that nobody would ever know about the 'little weight problem'. She also told Arvella that she was about to run out of time. She knew Ance might just come in if they released him from duty. It was about time for the army to let him out. He had been in Italy for two and half years and the army usually did not keep them three years. Vina said she had to get rid of 'the evidence', if you know what I mean, before Ance turned up back home. Well, it seems that some old woman from the bad section of town that works with Arvella got Vina hooked up with some old 'quack' doctor to get rid of 'her problem'. If you can believe this, Vina went through the night right by herself on a bus and found this all dingy light bulb on a light green door. That light was the signal that she was at the right place. The best I can gather is that this quack doctor, for a hundred dollar bill, would scrap out 'the evidence' and, right then and there, send the woman right straight back out on the street."

Tine caught her breath. "I never heard of such doings." She replied in dismay.

Osie gathered steam to finish the story, so she hastened the pace of her story to Tine because the stack of dishes was almost clean and dried.

"I cannot for the life of me figure out where in the world she got herself a hundred dollar bill. And, Arvella said, the daddy had to be from down here, but, she wouldn't even allow Arvella to speak of it as a baby, just "some weight" she had put on. Ain't that awful that she wouldn't admit it? That she would do such a thing as that? She would cheat on her man while he was over there fighting for his country and all, and not tell who the daddy is? Sounds like it may have belonged to a married man, don't it"? Osie barely caught her breath as she paid the narration to Tine.

Tine stayed mute. All day every time that she had looked at Vina she had noticed the dark pain behind Vina's eyes. Tine had noticed how Vina only talked when somebody said something straight to her. The rest of the time Vina had watched the children play and sometimes when Darla Faye whined, she would go gather her child up in her arms and carry her inside and rock her even if she were a small baby and her nearly a big old child now.

Tine wondered what she would have done if she had got with Oscar's child and her married to Bentley. She shuddered to think of what would have happened and who would have said what. Tine wondered what Bentley would have done if she had turned up expecting a baby. Bentley would have known a baby did not belong to him if she had a got in the family way by Oscar. Anyway it didn't happen to her. But, she wasn't a going pass judgment or carry on behind any woman's back after where she had been in all her weaknesses.

Those cousins who went to town were awful high and mighty talking about things like this. Tine would rather not hear a word of it. She did not like it when the women carried gossip back and forth about folks down home.

Osie continued, "Don't you ever say a word of what I just told you; but, I had to tell somebody. It is just seemed like a double sin in this family to me."

Tine thought to herself if Osie were counting on her to scatter gossip among the family, she was banking on the wrong person to do it.

Tine abruptly left the kitchen and hurried towards the front yard. As she rounded the corner of the house next to the dinner table, she called out.

"Drag the chairs up to the table now, girls, and let's all eat and talk all evening. We are not in a bit of a hurry now that the rest are all fed. Lordy, I have to have a piece of that three-tiered cake. That is a pretty thing. Is that sea foam icing? Who made that cake? How many egg whites did you use to make that anyway? Tell me how to make icing like that."

CHAPTER 22

After all the June vacationers from up North went home, and life settled back to routine. The gardens were laid by. Today a summer storm had been dumping rain like pouring sand out of out of a bucket the whole day long. Susie and Tine had been inside all day patching overalls and ironing up all the Sunday white shirts for Johnny and Bentley. Susie worked a while quilting on her double ring wedding quilt for her hope chest. Tine thought there will be a wedding here before fall. She could see it when Lester came calling on Susie. His eyes never left Susie the entire time even if he were talking with the men out in the shade after dinner, Tine had noticed. When she and Susie were cleaning up the dishes, Lester would sit in his chair where he could watch Susie through the kitchen door until she got her apron off and her bonnet on. When Susie came out in the yard, he was always eager to take her up on the walk out to the spring. They'd each take a bucket to get fresh water to drink for the afternoons on Sundays. Lester said he had never tasted water as good as from that black gum tree spring of everlasting water. Everybody that ever had a drink of water from that spring said that very same thing. It seemed that because the spring was up at the head of the holler all nested down under all them big pine trees in the shade, that that spring did more than give everlasting water.

It seemed like the whole ravine around that spring gave a body a renewed soul especially when one sat and rested a spell there.

Tine always sat down and rested a while at the black gum well.

Sometimes she remembered how Oscar and she had first touched and cried and made love all secured, it seemed, in that sweet cove. There were wonderful, precious little, chickadees that liked to peck around on pine cones there year round. Their little chirps were like the plucks of dulcimer strings singing praises to God. Tine loved to lie flat down on her back and gaze up at the sky or a while when she was there. Sometimes when she was resting there she wondered if she really would see Mommy and Eunice again and know them just like the Preacher Johnson said that everyone would know each other in heaven. She wondered how they'd really know one another if they didn't have no bodies and couldn't talk. She liked that scripture that said something about that people could only see through a glass darkly when it came to the spirits and things of God. I guess that meant a body wouldn't know the real truth until death came knocking on one's own door. Anyway, now that Mommy and Eunice were gone, she was not one bit afraid to die. Sometimes Tine wondered if these headaches and dizzy spells might eventually take her out this world. For some reason she couldn't really understand, Tine felt just like that Mommy and Eunice would be right there waiting to catch her whenever it was that she would fall from this good earth.

Sometimes at night when everyone else was asleep Tine knew she felt the presence of her mother with her. She could not prove one bit of what she felt. Old Granny Stanford had said to Tine's Mommy before Granny died that and her mommy came and visited her before she died. She swore it. Granny said over and over again that she saw all of them standing right there in big circles of the whitest light she'd ever seen. Granny said that they told her to come on to them. They called her by her name even. Tine's Mommy declared that Granny Stanford was in her right mind when she told them what she had seen and heard from the other world.

"Why in the world am I thinking on such stuff as this today?" Tine asked herself shaking her head.

Susie jumped at the loud bolt of thunder that shook the winders. "I swear I wish it would quit this rain." She complained.

Tine replied, "One time when I was a right big little girl, it rained seven days and seven nights. The mail mule didn't come. The logging train that runs along the river didn't get in and out for about ten or twelve days the water got so high. Everybody around here said it was the worst flood they had ever seen. All the houses along the river got water seven feet or so in them. Most of the folks pulled what stuff they had and stayed upstairs, if they had an upstairs. Some people just plum had to leave home and could not go back home at all until the water went back down. Seems like if I remember right, the air feels just like it did then for this last two or three days. Something about the air just does not feel right, though I can't rightly put my finger on what it is. The air is heavy, too heavy. Maybe we ought to get the cows in even if it raining. If we wait until milking time, that branch might get up so high we can't get them to the barn. Get Bentley's old coat and hat for me out of the side room and get Johnny's for you. We will go on and get them cows in early. We won't have to do the milking now though."

The four cows were hovering against the gap poles all grouped up in a bunch real close like with their backs against the blinding rain sheets and wind. Seems like animals always sensed when the weather was out of whack. The cows mooed right low in their throats as soon as Susie and Tine crossed the log foot bridge across the branch to the milk gap. The cows sounded as if they were asking them to come on and thanking them for a coming to put them in the barn out of the rain. Susie let down the poles at the gap in the fence from the top one to the bottom one. Old Jers, the leader, was the first one to lumber across the poles; in fact, she pushed herself right on through the gap while Susie was pulling down the last pole. The next one, a dry cow, pushed in right behind Jers; then, Brindle, the next fresh milker; then another dry cow followed; they sprinted across that rushing branch, twisted their tails and went lickety-split straight into the barn hallway.

The dry cows didn't usually get to come to the barn; but, Tine yelled to Susie as she came rushing to the barn behind Brindle, "Let them all stay in the barn tonight. The lightning is so bad they might get hit, especially if they huddle up under a tree like they do in a bad rain. That makes them twice as likely to get killed by a strike of lightning. I seen four hit at once and drop to their knees and die afore they hit the ground at my daddy's neighbor's house during a bad storm. They were all four standing under the same big oak tree a trying to take shelter from the weather. We can't take chances and this stormy weather shows no signs of a letting up anytime soon. If Bentley don't like it the way we are doing this and overrules us; he can let them out when he gets home. That way he can't lay it on us that we didn't take care of them."

They put each cow in a separate stall; then, Tine and Susie plodded through the muddy barn lot and splashed and splashed with ground water running over into their shoes. They bent low with their faces away from the torrents of rain. The run to the front porch ended in a rush. They shed their wet coats and hats and hung them over porch chairs to dry. Streams of water oozed out of them and ran in midget-like rivers onto the porch then off the edge into the yard. The wind and the rain pushed them in the living room door. As soon as they entered the house, they jerked off the wet shoes and stockings and set them by the fireplace to dry. Tine had struck a match and had lit a little gnat-smoke-like fire that morning to drive out the dampness. She had kept the fire going all day to knock out the chill from the perpetual storm.

About four o'clock, Johnny come in all soaked, too. He had been out the road with Pap. He and his Pap were good buddies. When Johnny had time he would go and sit with Pap and talk and he'd draw stuff for Pap. Pap said Johnny was a whole like Elmer except Elmer carved things out of wood instead of drawing like Johnny was always doing.

Tine instructed him as he came in, "John, pull off them wet boots and put them beside our shoes and let them dry awhile; then, so get the mop and mop up the rug or one of us will shore fall if you don't."

Johnny did as she instructed, but said as he mopped up the water, "I have not ever seen this much water running on the top of the ground in my life. Pap said that this rain just didn't seem right for this time of the year. I swear walking home on the road was like wading a shallow creek. The rain is coming down so fast the water can't get run off nowhere."

Tine answered him, "The branches, creeks will be out of their banks by nightfall if it don't let up. Bentley has to cross that river with his produce wagon on the way in. Let's hope he gets across it before it gets too flooded or he will have to stay on yon side of it, that's for certain. Hope he don't try to cross it if it's too deep. At least, if he had a good selling day; he'll be empty and won't loose any animals or produce. This time of year most of them folks in the mining camp will buy all the chickens and eggs and cured meat and canned stuff he can haul in one day. They don't have any garden stuff coming in yet and what they canned up, if they did can up last year's garden is gone by now.

"Maybe we ought to go on in a little while and milk them two cows out and feed early today," Tine calculated in a worried tone. "That rain is just a getting heavier all the time."

They waited until their shoes were about halfway dry; hunted some more dry coats; then, down towards dark, they all three wrapped up again and went to the barn. Susie took one cow. Tine took the other one. Johnny got corn out of the crib and put some in for the two dry cows and then he shelled a bucket full of corn off the cob on the hand corn sheller. He scattered the shelled corn out over the barn lot to the chickens and ducks. He threw several cobs across into the hog lot to feed the hungry pigs who rooted their corn cobs around in the mud while eating them right on in the rain. Then, he went down to the sheep pen and checked then out. The ewes had the lambs all in under the shelter. They were all bedded down like it was already night time.

Johnny toiled up the incline from the animal pens to the barn all stooped over. He did not look up all the way through the barn lot with his head bent low trying to shelter his face.

Susie's voice startled him. "Johnny, oh Johnny, come here quick! Momma is down and I can't get her up. Hurry, hurry! Oh God, Johnny, she has passed plum out!" Susie was screaming.

Johnny broke out into a limping run. When he got to the entrance to the hallway, Tine was a laying face first in the dirt. The bucket of hot milk was turned on its side and flowing down the hall way in rivulets. The cats were licking in it. Susie was down on her knees trying to turn Tine's body over face up.

"Momma, answer me! Momma, can you hear me? Oh, Momma, what is wrong?"

Susie was repeating over and over.

She turned her mother's face around and put her finger under her nose; then, put her ear to her mother's back to listen for Tine's breath or heartbeat.

"Johnny, Momma is out colder than kraut. I can feel her breathe but she won't answer me. When she opened the stall door with the full bucket of milk, she started a falling and when I saw that she was falling, I threwed my bucket down and started towards her; but, I couldn't catch her to save my life." Susie began crying fearfully.

"Johnny, run, run! You have got to go get Mam and Pap. Tell them to come on. Tell them that Momma has been a having dizzy spells. Tell them that this time she has passed out cold! Tell them to come quick and help us get her back to the house!" Susie instructed through her tears.

Johnny turned and started back out the road running as fast as his humped crooked back would allow him. He would run two steps then skip two steps, but he was intent on getting to Pap's for help as fast as his crippled self would carry him.

When Bentley got home he found Mam and Pap at the house and Johnny and Susie standing by Tine's bed crying. Tine was still all passed out completely and nothing they could do would bring her to. Mam and Pap stood helpless and confused too horrified to cry.

Bentley saddled the mare. He left in a hurry to go get Dr. Jed.

CHAPTER 23

That night, Dr. Jed spoke is a soft pleasant tone while still holding Tine's hand, "Clementine, Bentley told me that you are having problems with headaches and that your eyes are giving you problems seeing well. He told me that you have been dizzy and had some passing out spells according to the children. I am going to pull up a chair and sit and we will talk awhile. After we talk, I will take a light and look into your eyes and do an examination and ask you several questions. Bentley has already said I can spend the night here; so, we won't have to hurry."

Tine answered, Dr. Jed in a slow weak labored voice, "Of course, you can stay here. The girls will cook you a good breakfast in the morning. Make yourself at home. I am so glad you are here. I was a needing a good doctor. I put it off as long as I could. I am glad Bentley went to get you here to see me."

Dr. Jed began with his questions.

Tine narrated her symptoms to him. She did not forget to tell him about the times she was blacked out and almost went out of her head with pain after she came to herself. She told Dr. Jed that did not remember birthing Johnny.

Dr. Jed took a light and looked deep into Tine's eyes and down her throat and into her ears. He took his hands and pushed her head around in circles and from side to side. Tine winched and cried out in pain. When the good doctor turned Tine's head over to one side a big sharp pain ran all the way to the end of her fingers; and then, her arm went numb. Dr. Jed made some notes in his little black book. When he finished his examination and notes he sat down in the chair beside Tine's bed. He put his head in his hands. After a few minutes of silence, Dr. Jed spoke in a comforting professional tone.

"Tine, I have some serious things to tell you. Do you want me to tell you in here with just you for do you want Bentley and, or any or all of the children in here with you?"

Tine did not have to have the doctor to tell her that she was sick unto death. She already knew. "Tell me whatever you want to tell me. Then, you can go tell the others. I just want to know how long you think I will last. Can you give me anything for the pain when it gets the worst? Sometimes, I throw up my head hurts so."

"Well, Clementine, what I think is wrong is that you have a brain tumor. It is pretty far progressed. I don't know how long it will take; but cancer may well be in its final stages. I think you have had it since your very first headaches and dizzy spells, maybe as far back as before Johnny was born. I would guess a few months is the time left that you have; but, only God holds those answers. Yes, I can give you pain killers to take by mouth. When you get in the final stages, I will come and give your morphine shots to help with your suffering. You are a strong and brave woman, lady," Dr. Jed pronounced.

"A body has to take whatever they are dished out, Dr. Jed. I feel like I can sleep awhile; my pain has not been so bad today it seems like. I rest when I can. Go tell Bentley and the children, will you?"

With those words, Tine drifted off to sleep. She dreamed she was at the black gum well for water washing her face over and over again in the cooling waters. At times she mumbled unrecognizable words in her sleep.

After Dr. Jed had watched Tine ease into restful sleep, he left her in the total quietness of the room. He went into the kitchen and sat at the kitchen table and awaited Sally's (who had come home to help take care of Tine) pouring his coffee; "black" was his only comment when Sally offered to fill his cup. He sipped away at his coffee; then, he asked Sally to call the family into the living room by the fire.

"I would like to talk to you all at once," he requested.

Sally moved to gather the family in around the fireplace. Johnny came from his drawing in the lower room where Susie quilted away beside him. Bentley was out on the front porch just rocking away in the night air. It was midnight. At Sally's request for the family to gather in to listen to Dr. Jed, all of them moved in slow motion to the living room where each sat in a hickory bark-bottomed chair. Dr. Jed entered from the kitchen and took the rocking chair that had a cushioned seat. He searched the faces of each person in the room and then simply stated: "Dear ones, Tine is not going to live very much longer."

Susie gasped and covered her mouth with both hands. Sally let tears slid down her face and lifted her apron tail to dab them. Johnny's hands trembled.

Bentley just hung his head a few moments; then, he raised up and looked straight at Dr. Jed who explained to them as they listened intently, "I think that she has had a brain tumor for a long time now; it probably was there before Johnny was born. The extra drain on her system is probably why the pregnancy and birthing were so difficult for her. She asked me to tell you all. Tine knows already that she has limited days. She is one strong woman; a well of inspiration to me. She has shown great strength to have kept on going and working and not complaining, mostly suffering for years, in silence, I assume. Tine told me that she feels just like a tree that is planted by the waters and for me to tell you all and the other children that it won't be long until she will be crossing over Jordan. She wants for you all not to worry at all about her now. I think the best thing to do for her is to keep her still and quiet. Let only a few that she loves come in and see her for a short visit now and then, when she feels up to having visitors. I will leave her pain pills and when she gets in the final hours."

"How long?" Bentley asked with a deep quiver in his voice.

"Can't tell, maybe fifteen or twenty days, at the most, I suspect," Dr. Jed made the statement.

Bentley glanced at Sally and commanded, "Write Oscar to come on home."

With that Bentley went to the kitchen, took him a drink out of the gourd dipper and lifted his hat off the wooden peg by the kitchen door. He picked up the water bucket and headed to the black gum well. At the black gum well before he filled the bucket, Bentley got down on his knees and began to cry. He let out wails of tearful pain fall over the water as it spilled over the sides of the hollow log well drum.

He cried out in agony, "What will I do without Tine? Lord, you said that you give and take away; but, Lord, why are you a taking her now before Johnny gets all growed up and before Susie has a home of her own and all established and stuff. I don't know what to do and no woman. Lord, help us. Lord, help the children give up their mother. Lord, help me to help the children someway. And, Lord, I am so afraid without Tine. She is my help mate. Lord, let her stay awhile longer. Heal her if you would."

When his body became weak from his crying and pleading with God, he set the water bucket and let it fill to the brim. Then, he bent his face over the gushing well and splashed the cooling waters upon his face in huge overflowing handfuls bathing his swollen eyes until they felt clear. He lifted his bucket of fresh water and headed to the house. He needed to sit with Tine; and, he wanted to be with the children. Bentley stumbled weakly with the gait of an old man towards the house.

Dr. Jed had told Tine that eventually her right eye would go blind. Tine noted that in the last two or three days that she could not tell who was who when they entered her side bed room to ask her if she needed anything. She decided not to tell Bentley or the children or any of the other folks that she was not seeing very well and did not know who came to take turns sitting up with her unless he or she spoke to her.

Dr. Jed also told her that the pain would become so bad that she, most likely, would not know every much about anything that was going on around her during the final days. He had left morphine for her to have when she asked for it.

Thus far Tine was able to bear the pain alone. Sometimes she found herself moaning when the worst strikes came. She had noticed that her tongue and neck felt numb and that all her food tasted alike, flat and flavorless. She swallowed it anyway to feed her ailing body. She did not want to worry anyone any worse than they already were. Johnny was the one she hated to die and leave the worst especially with his back growing more and more disfigured and with how clumsy he had become. Tine had noticed that Johnny had fallen over in the corner the other day when he reached to get a towel off the head board to wipe the sweat off her brow during one of the bad pain attacks. She wondered sometimes if he didn't hurt as badly as she did; but, her boy, Johnny, never complained one compliant. He just tried his best to help the girls and Bentley ever way he could. He never missed his turn sitting with her.

One morning Tine woke up with her bad eye clear enough for her to see real good. She did not feel pain in the side of her head. She got out of bed and dressed herself, reached for the walking stick that Bentley had whittled out of a young maple sapling for her to use to steady herself when she felt weak and trembling if she tried walking very far.

Tine sat down at the kitchen table beside Johnny who was drawing a team of mules on his drawing pad. She reached over and patted his drawing hand.

"John, lay down your pencil and go with me to the black gum well. I can't go without you. I might not make it back to the house or I might fall and not be able to get back up by myself."

Tine slowly raised herself up to take her son's arm. She left the cane leaning against the chair.

159

"Johnny, let's go to the black gum well."

Today she would lean on Johnny.

When they arrived at the spring, Johnny, said to his mother, "Mom, would you like to sit by the spring awhile? I will walk on out to Pap's and see if him and Mam need any of us to help them do anything this week. You will be fine until I get back, won't you?" Without waiting for an answer to his own question, Johnny finished his statements with a request.

"Don't you try to get up and walk? Just lay back on the moss there and enjoy yourself."

Before dust set in, Johnny led his mother back to the house by allowing her to lean heavily on him. Tine heard Bentley come into the kitchen with two buckets of water from the well. Bentley sat down at the kitchen table. It was almost dark. The girls had gone to shut the chicken house door and the cellar door and to double check the smoke house door. They would be back to clear the table and wash up the dishes after their daddy had finished his supper.

Tine had tried to eat; but, couldn't seem to swallow a bite. The meat tasted like cardboard to her dry tongue. She left her plate on the table beside her bed after one bite.

All of a sudden, she heard Bentley shove his chair back. The chair fell and hit the wall against the part of the kitchen that shared the petition of the wall beside her bed. First, she trembled, then, she froze. Her right eye was being very blurred and her entire face was swollen. The pain over her eye was all of a sudden throbbing. The balls of light were streaming across the eyeballs like zigzagging miniature lightning streaks.

Tine, alarmed at the noise the chair had made, cocked her head sideways intent on hearing what was going on in the kitchen.

She overheard Johnny began in a trembling voice, "My hand just did not have enough strength to hold onto the handle it just gave out. My back was sending pain right down my arms into my hands. I should have got just one bucket at a time so I could have held onto it.

I will mop it up. Just let me mop it up. Where's the mop? Where's that mop. I will mop it up and then go get another bucket from the well," Johnny kept repeating to his father.

Bentley did not hear his apology.

"Ain't I told you no better than that? Can't you figure one thing out on your own?"

Are you just slouching off and playing sorry ass with that back because you want to draw all the time instead of work like a man? Does somebody have to draw a circle in the sand to show you what to do? You just seem slow and not ever been as quick on the uptake as your older brothers? What do you aim to do when your mommy is gone and not here to always take up for you and give excuse for your slouching off and making dumb mistakes like spilling a gallon of water all over the floor for them girls to clean up with them already almost killed from standing on their feet cooking and cleaning? Now you just caused them triple work." Bentley shouted without pause.

Johnny stuttered, "But-but I will clean it up myself if I had the mop."

Bentley stomped to the bedroom and took his razor strap off the wall; then, turned in a lurch toward the kitchen, he began bellowing out, "Come in here boy, where are you? Where'd you go? You can't hide from me? I will give you twice as many licks if you don't get in this kitchen and take this medicine. This razor strap will teach you good!"

Tine lunged with all her strength and threw her legs over the side of the bed. She stood up. Her world spun around and around. She could only see out of her left eye. The right one had all of a sudden gone completely black. She felt for the straight chair back and took hold of the top of it as if it were a walker. She steadied herself with the chair and inched forward toward the kitchen. Her knees trembled. Her ankles warbled. She inched forward toward Bentley's voice until she reached the open doorway to the kitchen; then, she stood still.

Johnny was entering the back door with the mop in his hand. He was headed to mop up the spilled water. As Johnny entered the kitchen,

Bentley leaped toward him and grabbed him by the arm. He started slinging Johnny around and around him in a circle beating him in long hash lashes with the razor strap. The licks that Bentley struck out were synchronized with each lurch that Johnny made. Bentley was twice as tall and twice as strong as Johnny; he kept slinging him in a circle for at least fifteen quick circles and giving a lash per circle. On the last circle, Bentley slipped in the spilled water and lost his grip on Johnny's arm. Johnny fell head first in behind the door that was open back from the living room to the kitchen. He scrambled up onto his feet and grabbed a hold of the door knob to try to make a triangle of safety from the beating. Johnny, as if by instinct, realized that he could use the mop as a weapon. As his father started lashing at the door with only the ends of the strap lacing stripes across Johnny's thighs. Johnny shoved the mop handle with all his power deep into the folds of his father's fat belly.

Tine fell forward towards the kitchen table and caught the edge of it and held on with both hands. She pulled herself up to lean against the table. She picked up Bentley's coat off the back of his chair. With all the power left in her ailing body, she slapped Bentley's back over and over again with his folded coat.

Bentley looked wild-eyed and stunned at the mop handle in Johnny's hands that had gouged into his stomach and at the limp coat in Tine's hands.

Bentley stood motionless and speechless.

Tine's voice was weakened by the damage of her brain cancer. She began to speak in a low even voice, "Bentley, turn around and hit me. Hit me. I am about gone anyway. Hit me. I don't care. You always hit the children or the animals when you fly off like this. What in this world causes you to loose your mind sometimes? I have tried to be a good wife and keep my mouth shut and help my children deal with you and your wild spells. I never do know when you are a going go into one of them of these crazy beating you do or why on earth you do such a thing. Johnny told you he did not mean to spill that water. Johnny told you that he would mop it up; but, you didn't even hear him, just like you don't ever hear a word that anybody says whilst you are in the midst of them beating spells. Did your daddy beat on you all? Well, if you had half a mind, you'd know it is not right. The Bible says that you should love your neighbor as yeself. Well, before I die, Bentley, I want you to know that I believe that God thinks that a man's children and his wife are his neighbors. You wouldn't ever think of laying a hand on the neighbors or any other child you know; so, why in the world do you hit on your children? If a man loves his family just like he loves his self, he wouldn't beat on them for no reason. You don't beat up on yourself not once. Well, Bentley, it is about time you quit your beatings. Johnny is sick. Dr. Jed said it is a real unusual thing that is wrong with him and that it will not be going away and that it may get worse. There is no cure for him. Johnny will never be able to work like a real man. I want you to promise me here tonight while I can still hear you that you will stop this nonsense that someway you will get a hold of yourself and never lay a hand on Johnny again. I wish to God I would had enough strength to call your hand the first time you ever hit on one of the children; but, my daddy told me that you were a good man with a good name and a hard worker and that you would provide for a family and that you would stand by us. Bentley, you are hard worker. You don't mean to do bad things. Deep in your heart I think that you are a God fearing man. You had better stop and think about what you are doing sometimes. The neighbors and the family don't have a single idea of how you treat your children when you loose your temper over some stupid thing that doesn't make a lick of sense. Promise me, Bentley! Promise me now that you won't strike Johnny again."

Johnny had moved to the kitchen table. Johnny had folded over on the kitchen table, his head in his hands, and he was sobbing uncontrollable. His rib cage shook up and down; up and down until he would gag; then, he would fall into his sobbing again. Johnny never looked up. Snot ran out of his nose and onto his hands. He did not bother to wipe it away.

Tine continued, "Give me the razor strop, Bentley. Give it to me now. I am not going to hit you with it. I couldn't hurt you anyway. I am too weak. You are going to suffer inside all your life over the way you have hurt my children."

In slow motion, Bentley laid the razor strop on the table. He picked up his jacket and went out the back door into the night. Tine picked up the razor strap and instructed Johnny: *"Take that blasted thing and burn it in the fire."* Johnny obliged his mother.

Then, he turned and went to his mother and slipped his arm around her waist. He was limping. He steadied himself as his mother leaned against his frail shoulder and she slipped her arm around him.

"Momma, let me help you back to your bed," he offered in a comforting, yet shaky tone. Slowly in even paced steps, he ushered his ailing mother across the water- slick floor and into the bedroom. After Tine lay down, he lifted her covers and placed them up around her shoulders. Johnny bent down and lightly kissed her on the cheek, then whispered in her ear, "I love my momma; I love my momma."

Johnny sat in the bark-bottomed straight chair beside his mother's bed and watched her fall into a fitful doze. He heard the back door close. He heard his father mopping up the spilled water on the kitchen floor.

Bentley kept on mopping until all the water was cleaned up. He hung the mop on the line on the back porch to dry. He went into the living room and sat down in the rocking chair. He took his handkerchief out of his pocket and wiped away the tears that were oozing out of the corners of his eyes.

Johnny continued to sit beside his mother. He did not draw any that night. As Johnny sat beside his mother's bed and listened to her labored breathes grow as weak as a little puny baby chicken's.

CHAPTER 24

The next morning at ten o'clock, someone knocked on the front door. Sally opened it surprised to find her Uncle Oscar standing there with his hat in his hand.

She turned and yelled out, "Uncle Oscar is here!" She hugged his neck and said Dad is at the barn. Come on in. Come on in."

"Did you ride the bus home?" Sally inquired.

"Would like a cup of coffee?" She added.

"Yes, I rode the bus all night to get here. I left the day I got the letter that Tine was sick. No, I don't need coffee. Is your mommy real bad?" Sally's head hung down in and she nodded affirmation to his question.

Oscar stood quiet and swallowed read hard. The corners of his mouth twitched with unspoken grief. His hands trembles ever so slightly, as he said to Sally, "I will go on over to the barn to see Bentley."

Dawn broke the next morning with a cool drizzle dampening the window panes. Tine lay motionless and silent. She thought she heard a bunch of women singing, "Yes, we will gather at the river, the beautiful, beautiful river"...All of a sudden through the swirls of darkness a white light, bright as a July morning sun on a clear day beamed into her eyes. Tine reached her hands upward. She thought she was easing her fingers against the rounded worn wet-black well drum. The water spilled over the sides of the wooden well and sparkled like wet spider webs being illuminated with early morning September sun rays. Tine felt the cooling rivulets tickle the entire length of her up righted arms. Soft drops of the pure moisture oozed off her elbows like early morning dew before the sun rose and swiped them away.